"You're on my boat. Leave. Now."
Tightening her fist, she jabbed at
him again, but his forearm blocked
her. It was like pushing against steel.

He made some sound, almost like a bored sigh.
"You really don't want to do that, sweet cheeks,"
he muttered, disarming her as easily as drawing
breath. As if he fought off women for a living.
Then his hand loosened, skated down her raised
arm, from wrist to elbow and she didn't doubt
that was exactly what he did—and on a daily
basis.

"You're on my boat," she repeated, but it came
out like more of a whisper.

"Yet I have key."

Before she could analyze that drily delivered fact
or think of a response, he released her, stepped
sideways and flipped on the light switch. Then
he raised both hands to show he meant no harm.

She blinked as her eyes adjusted to the sudden
glare.

Blake Everett.

She sagged against the table, but her relief
was quickly chased away by a different kind of
tension.

When not teaching or writing, **ANNE OLIVER** loves nothing more than escaping into a book. She keeps a box of tissues handy—her favorite stories are intense, passionate, against-all-odds romances. Eight years ago, she began creating her own characters in paranormal and time-travel adventures, before turning to contemporary romance. Other interests include quilting, astronomy, all things Scottish and eating anything she doesn't have to cook. Sharing her characters' journeys with readers all over the world is a privilege…and a dream come true. Anne lives in Adelaide, South Australia, and has two adult children. Visit her website, www.anne-oliver.com. She loves to hear from readers. Email her at anne@anne-oliver.com.

Other titles by Anne Oliver available in ebook:

Harlequin Presents Extra

THERE'S SOMETHING ABOUT A REBEL...

ANNE OLIVER

~ Risky Business ~

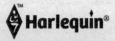

TORONTO NEW YORK LONDON
AMSTERDAM PARIS SYDNEY HAMBURG
STOCKHOLM ATHENS TOKYO MILAN MADRID
PRAGUE WARSAW BUDAPEST AUCKLAND

Recycling programs
for this product may
not exist in your area.

ISBN-13: 978-0-373-52852-3

THERE'S SOMETHING ABOUT A REBEL...

First North American Publication 2012

THERE'S SOMETHING
ABOUT A REBEL...

CHAPTER ONE

IT WASN'T the rumble of approaching thunder that woke Lissa Sanderson some time after midnight. Nor was it Mooloolaba's tropical heat that had prompted her to leave the houseboat's windows open to catch whatever breeze was coming off the river. It wasn't even her seriously serious financial situation that had kept her tossing and turning for the past few weeks.

It was the sound of footsteps on her little jetty.

Unfamiliar footsteps. Not her brother's—Jared was overseas, and no one she knew would be calling in at this ridiculously unsociable hour. A shiver scuttled down her spine.

Lifting her head off the pillow, she heard the leafy palm fronds around the nearby pool clack together and the delicate tinkle of her wind chimes over the back door as the sound of approaching footsteps drew closer. Heavy and slow but with a sense of purpose.

Her thoughts flashed back nine months to Todd and ice slid through her veins. The Toad wouldn't be game to show his face in this part of the world again. Would he? No. He. Would. *Not*.

Swinging her legs over the side of her bed, she scanned the familiar gloom for her heavy-duty marine torch then remembered she'd used it to check the new leak in the ceiling and left it in the galley. *Damn it*.

The jetty belonged to the owners of the luxury riverside home that was rented to wealthy holiday-makers, but her lease on the private dock wasn't up for another two years. February was low season and the house had been vacant for the past couple of weeks. Maybe new tenants had arrived and were unaware that the jetty was off-limits?

That had to be it. 'Please let that be it,' she murmured.

The carport she used to gain access through the back yard and from there to her boat was security coded—who else could it be? She told herself not to overreact. Not to give in to the unease that had stalked her these past months. Both doors were secure, windows open but locked. Mobile phone beside her bed, both Jared and her sister, Crystal, on speed dial.

The footsteps stopped. A weighted thump vibrated through the floor, tilting it ever so slightly beneath her feet for a second or two. The resulting ripple of water lapped against the hull and the hairs on the back of her neck prickled.

Someone was on her deck. Right outside her door.

Okay, now she could be officially scared. She pushed up, grabbing her mobile and punching in numbers, then stared at the black screen. No charge. *Great. Just great.* Heart galloping, she darted to the bedroom doorway. From here she had a clear view down the length of the boat to the glass door where a light drizzle sheened the deck—and the stranger.

Tall. Male. His outline glistening with moisture.

Too broad-shouldered for Todd, thank God, but it could have been the hunchback of Notre Dame, his silhouette sharpening as silvery sheet lightning edged in bronze flickered behind him.

In the clammy air her skin chilled.

Then the hunch lifted away from his shoulders and she realised it was some kind of duffle bag. She pressed a fist to her mouth to stifle the hysteria rising up her throat. The bag or whatever-it-was hit the deck with a scuffed thud, then he straightened to a height and breadth rivalling her brother's and she drew back instinctively. The sound in her throat turned to a choked gasp.

She swallowed it down. Even as she told herself that it was probably a new arrival checking out the grounds, she was pulling on her dressing gown, yanking the sash tight. She pocketed the useless phone.

She could exit via the rear door near her bed, but to leave the boat she'd have to pass within a close couple of steps of him on the narrow jetty then make it past the pool to the carport, wait for the roller door to rise… Safer to remain where she was.

And if he wasn't a new arrival… *How had he managed to get past the security-coded roller door?*

Because he knew the code, right? Right. The thought was reassuring. Still, she had to force one foot in front of the other, her bare feet soundless over the linoleum as she skirted boxes and crates until she slipped on a pool of moisture that hadn't been there a couple of hours earlier. Arms flailing and swearing to herself, she came to a slippery stop in her tiny galley, gripped the edge of her equally tiny table and looked outside.

His sheer size swamped her deck. A flash of lightning revealed black clothing, bare forearms and uncompromising features. Alarmingly good-looking for a potential burglar. *Vaguely familiar.* Short black hair silvered with raindrops, dark stubbled square jaw. Big hands as he patted his chest then slid them down the front of his thighs as if he'd lost something.

Dangerous. The errant thought of those hands patting her own chest sent an unwelcome thrill rippling down her spine. Something shimmered at the edge of her earliest teenage memories. A guy. As out of reach and dangerous and darkly beguiling as this man…

She shook old images away. She'd been fooled by one too many tall-dark-and-handsomes to be fooled again. And this man was probably looking for his lock pick while she was standing here like a loon and letting him, when what she *should* have been doing was phoning the police. With her dead phone.

Her limbs went into lock-down while her slow-motion brain tried—and failed—to figure her next move. She could smell the calming scents of the jasmine candle she'd used earlier, the fresh basil she'd picked and put in a jar on the sink, the ever-present pervasive river.

Would they be her last memories before she died?

She watched, frozen, while he dug into a trouser pocket and pulled something out then stepped right up to the door.

Adrenaline spurted through her veins, propelling her into action. Reaching for the nearest object—a seashell the size of her fist—she curled stiff fingers between its reassuring spikes and stood as tall as her five feet three inches would allow.

'Go away. This is private pr—'

Her pitifully thin demand was gulped over a dry mouth when she heard the heart-stopping click of a *key* being turned in the lock. The door slid open and the stranger stepped inside, bumping into her brass wind chime on the way and bringing the fragrance of rain with him.

She yanked her phone from her pocket. 'No closer.' His silhouette loomed darkly as he moved and her nostrils flared at the potent smell of wet male. 'I've called the police.'

He came to an abrupt halt. She sensed surprise but no fear and she realised her voice had given her away. Female.

All-alone female.

She lunged forward, the makeshift weapon in her other hand aimed at his throat. She felt the pressure as the shell's prongs met flesh.

Before she could draw breath, his arm blocked hers. 'Easy. I'm not going to hurt you.' His deep voice accompanied the thunder that rolled across the ocean.

'I don't know that.' And she wasn't giving him the chance.

'You're on my boat. Leave. *Now.*' Tightening her fist on her shell, she jabbed at him again but his forearm blocked her. It was like pushing against steel.

He made some sound, like an almost bored sigh. 'You really don't want to do that, sweet cheeks,' he muttered, disarming her as easily as drawing breath. As if he fought off women for a living. Then his hand loosened, skated down her upraised arm from wrist to elbow and she didn't doubt that was exactly what he did—and on a daily basis.

The limb that no longer seemed to belong to her remained within the heat of his hand *of its own volition*, while hot and cold shivers chased over her skin. 'You're on my boat,' she repeated, but it came out like more of a whisper.

'Yet I have a key.'

Before she could analyse that dryly delivered fact or think of a response, he released her, stepped sideways and flipped on the light switch. Then he raised both hands to show her he meant no harm.

She blinked as her eyes adjusted to the sudden glare. As she noticed the red mark where the shell had grazed a bronzed neck. As her brain caught up with the fact that yes, absolutely, he had a key and he'd reached for the light switch with such easy familiarity...

Blake Everett.

She sagged against the table but her partial relief was quickly chased away by a different kind of tension. He wore faded black jeans and a black sweater washed almost transparent with age. The shrunken sleeves ended halfway down thick sinewy forearms sprinkled with dark masculine hair.

Jared's mate. Her first innocent crush when she'd been nine years of age and he'd been eighteen and joined the navy. Then when he'd come home on leave after his mother's death...oh, my... She'd been thirteen to his twenty-two but she'd looked at him as a woman would, dreamed of him as only a woman would and she'd kept the guilty pleasure a secret.

She doubted he'd ever looked at her other than the time she'd fallen off her skateboard trying to impress him and bloodied her nose, his whiter-than-white T-shirt and, most of all, her young pride.

Gossip had circulated. *Bad boy. Black sheep.* It hadn't changed the way she thought of him until eventually she heard the rumours that he'd got Janine Baker pregnant then skipped town to join the navy. In an odd way, she'd felt betrayed.

He had eyes that could turn from tropical-island blue to glacial in an instant and an intense brooding aloofness that had called to her feminine nurturing side even way back then. She'd spent a lot of time imagining what it would be like to be the focus of all that intensity.

And now...maybe now he was looking at her the way she'd always wanted him to...with a definite glint of heat in those summertime eyes. But where men were concerned, she wasn't as naïve now. And she wasn't looking back—not *that* way. Absolutely not. She wasn't thirteen any more and there was a major problem here.

'My name's Blake Everett,' he said into the silence broken only by an intermittent *plop* of water leaking from the roof into a plastic container on the floor. He remained where he was, hip propped easily against her counter top, his gaze skimming her too-slinky too-skimpy dressing gown and making her tingle from head to foot before meeting her eyes once more. 'I—'

'I know who you are.' Posture stiff, she resisted the urge to hug her arms across her braless breasts to hide her suddenly erect *traitorous* nipples. She concentrated on relaxing tense muscles. Shoulders, neck, hands. *Breathe.*

His gaze turned assessing, then stern, drawing her attention to the pallor beneath the tanned complexion, the heavy lines of fatigue around his eyes and mouth. But his lips... They were still the most sensual lips she'd ever laid eyes on—full, firm, luscious—

'You're one up on me, then.'

At his clipped reply, she dragged her wayward eyes up to his. He didn't recognise her. *Good.* 'So now we're even.'

He frowned. 'How do you figure that?'

She knew him? Ignoring the cramped muscles from the rain-lashed drive up from Surfers and the headache battering away inside his skull, Blake searched his memory while he studied her. No hardship there.

He hadn't been this close to a woman in a while, let alone one as attractive as this little redhead. After the navy's testosterone-fuelled environment, she smelled like paradise. In the yellow light her hair shone brighter than a distress flare and her eyes were the clear translucent green of a tropical lagoon, but, just as the pristine-looking beaches he routinely assessed hid potential and possibly lethal dangers, there was a storm brewing behind that gaze.

And no wonder—the old man had obviously neglected to inform her that it wasn't his boat to rent out. Ten years ago when his mother had died, Blake had bought it from him to help get his father out of debt and to secure himself a quiet and solitary place to stay when he was on leave in Australia. He'd not been back since.

'I understand if you're renting. I've been overseas and my father—'

'I'm *not* renting. My brother bought this boat from your dad three years ago. It belongs to our family now. This is my home so…so you'll need to find somewhere else.'

'Your brother bought the boat…' He remembered the less-than-considered transaction and an ominous foreboding tracked up his spine. He should've known better than to trust a gambling addict—

'Jared Sanderson.'

Jared? The familiar name spoken in that stiletto-sharp voice sliced through his thoughts and he looked her over more thoroughly. The tousled bedroom hair, those aquamarine eyes and luxurious lips pulled down at the corners as she stared back at him. He'd lost contact with his long-time surfing buddy but he remembered the little sister…

'You're Melissa.' Still tiny in stature but all grown up and curvaceous and looking…different from the kid he remembered. Disturbingly so. Blood pumped a tad faster through his veins. *Don't go there.*

He flicked his eyes back to hers, catching a glimpse of generous breasts and smooth ivory décolletage on the way, before she jammed her arms in front of her. He didn't miss the remnant shadows in her gaze. 'I apologise for scaring you, Melissa. I should've knocked.'

'It's Lissa now. And yes, you should have.'

Her mouth pouted in that sulky way he remembered but tonight, rather than amused, he found himself oddly captivated. 'Lissa.'

She seemed to shake off the sulk. 'Okay, you just stripped five years off my life but apology accepted. And I didn't ring the police.' She lifted one delicate shoulder and gave a wry grimace. 'Phone's dead.' She blinked up at him, still wary. 'So what are you doing here?'

'A man can't come home after fourteen years?' He didn't elaborate. Now was not the time to ponder the demons that had sent him home to re-evaluate the universe and his place and purpose in it.

She shook her head. 'I mean what are you doing *here*, on the houseboat?'

'I thought I *owned* the houseboat.' Conned by his own father. He clenched his jaw. He should have made the effort to see his old man earlier today before driving up here but he hadn't needed the inevitable angst it would've entailed.

'No. You can't…' She frowned, confusion adding to the clouds in her eyes. 'I don't understand.'

'It's a long complicated story.' He rubbed absently at the tiny scratch beneath his chin.

'I'm sorry…about that.' She glanced at his throat and a pretty pink colour swam into her cheeks. 'I'll just get some—'

'Don't bother. I'm fine.'

But he didn't push the point as he watched her move to a cupboard and reach up…and up… Her shell-pink dressing gown grazed the tops of her thighs. Sleek, firm, creamy thighs that looked as if they'd been kissed by the sun.

Kissed. The word conjured a scenario he was better off not dwelling on but his lips tingled nonetheless. He ogled her spectacular rear without apology while she dragged out a box with assorted medication and pulled out a tube.

'This should…' She turned, catching him staring. He did not look away. It was the best view he'd seen in a long time. The colour in her cheeks intensified, bleeding into her throat. She thrust the tube at him, then, as if mortally afraid of skin contact, set it on the table beside them. 'There you go.'

'Thanks.'

She hesitated, as if finding the last minute or so discomforting in the extreme and determined to banish it from her mind, then said, 'Your long complicated story…I'm listening.'

He let out a slow breath, then said, 'Tomorrow I'll go back to Surfers, sort it out with Dad then discuss it with Jared. It'll be okay,' he assured her. He'd reimburse his old friend for the money he'd paid and help Melissa—Lissa—find alternative accommodation.

'It'll be okay, how? Jared purchased the boat when your father sold the home in Surfers and moved south. New South Wales, I think… No one knows exactly…'

It didn't come as a surprise. He acknowledged being left to discover the news about his father's apparent disappearance through another party with a shrug. 'I guess I already knew that.'

He'd paid his father cash for the boat the day he left

Australia, but he'd not actually signed anything...and the paperwork had never followed as promised.

When Blake had rung to query it, he discovered the phones had been disconnected and the emails began bouncing back... The old man hadn't been above using his son to suit his own purposes. Again, no surprise there.

'So...am I right then in assuming you own the house too?' She waved a hand towards the window. Outside, the predicted storm had set in. The rain had turned into a downpour, partially obscuring the view and pelting the roof and decking.

He nodded. He'd purchased what had been the family's luxury holiday house when he'd bought the houseboat. He'd gone through the bank to finance the deal and had the land title for that, at least, safely locked away.

'So why opt for the houseboat tonight when you have a more than adequate alternative?' she asked with a frown.

Despite having employed a service to stock the fridge and air the linen, he'd been unable to find the relaxation he needed to recuperate in the house. Too much space, too many rooms. Too many memories.

He'd lugged an old army bedroll he'd found in storage down to the waterfront hoping the familiar marine environment and solitude would help with the infernal headaches he'd suffered since the accident that had brought him back to Australia. Seemed he'd lucked out in both instances there too.

'I was hoping to catch up on some sleep.' He'd *not* expected to find a bed mate.

Her eyes widened, a hint of panic in their depths as they met his. 'But since I'm here already, you're going back up to the house, right?'

That had been his initial intention. Except...now his immediate plans for the night had been dashed he found he wasn't as tired as he'd thought and in no immediate hurry to bid the lovely Lissa Sanderson goodnight.

No, that wasn't quite correct, he decided. His *body* was

telling him to stay and get reacquainted, to absorb that feminine scent until his pores were saturated, to touch her arm again and feel that soft skin against his. His *body* had very definite ideas about where it wanted the evening to go.

His head was saying something else entirely.

His *head* didn't lead him astray. His diving team knew his reputation for remaining cool under pressure even in the most perilous situations.

Women were more likely to describe him as emotionally detached right before they slammed a door of some description in his face.

Either way, that was why he was good at his job and why he knew that Lissa Sanderson with her feminine curves and clear-eyed gaze that seemed to know exactly where his thoughts were going was trouble best avoided. For both parties.

Steeling himself for a restless night, he focused on that gaze. 'Okay, I'll leave you in peace. For now.'

'For *now*?' She stared at him, eyes huge and incredulous. 'This is *my home*.' Desperation scored her voice. 'You don't understand…I *need* this place.'

'Calm down, for heaven's sake.' Women. Always overreacting. 'We'll sort something out.' He glanced about him for the first time, remembering how the boat had looked years ago when his father had owned it. When Blake had lived on it.

Now a blue couch sagging beneath the weight of a jumble of boxes—some open, others taped shut—sat where there'd once been a leather lounge suite. Except for the addition of a microwave, the galley remained unchanged. If you didn't count the slather of paperwork on the bench. His gaze snagged on a final notice for payment for something or other attached to the fridge door with a magnet. *None of his business*.

Every square centimetre of the boat was crammed with stuff. Canvases against the wall beside an old tin of artists' brushes, another of charcoals and pencils. The bunk beds beyond were covered in swatches of fabric, colour palettes, magazines, wallpaper books. How did anyone live amidst such chaos?

Maybe it was the calming floral scents that pervaded the air or the potted herbs on a shelf near the window, but somewhere beneath the domestic carnage the place had a...comfortable cosiness. He'd not experienced anything like it since he'd been a youngster living with his mum, and wondered grimly if he could find sleep here after all.

He should leave the area entirely. Find somewhere else to rent along the coast somewhere while he was in Oz and forget he'd ever seen Melissa Sanderson. Solitude was what he wanted. What he craved until he felt halfway sane again.

A steady drip nearby diverted his attention, a silver tear-drop followed quickly by another against the light, and he glanced up. Obviously the leak had been there for some time judging by the half-full container beneath it. He'd been too preoccupied with everything else to notice. Now he scanned other damp patches. 'How long's this been going on?'

She glanced up at the ceiling, then away. 'Not long. I can manage, it's nothing.' Instantly defensive.

Interesting. If he remembered correctly, the young Melissa had been anything but independent. Or so it had seemed. 'Nothing? Look up, sweet cheeks. If water gets into that light socket there we've got a problem.'

He saw her glance up, then frown. Clearly she hadn't noticed the extent of the damage. He looked at the puddle near her feet lapping around the base of the fridge. 'Don't you know electricity and water don't mix?'

'Of course I do,' she snapped. 'And it's *I've* got a problem, not *we*.'

He shook his head. 'Right now I don't care whose problem it is, the boat's unsafe—for any number of reasons.' Now he'd seen the potential disaster he couldn't in all good conscience just leave her here to fend for herself and go back to bed, could he?

As if to make a point, a flash sizzled the air, accompanied by one almighty crash of thunder that reverberated between his ears in time with his throbbing head.

'That's it.' He rapped impatient knuckles on the table. 'Two minutes to grab what you need. You're sleeping in the house.'

CHAPTER TWO

'I BEG your pardon?' Lissa glared at him. It was hard to glare when faced with such gorgeousness, but she was through taking orders. From anyone. Ever again. 'I'm no—'

'Your choice, Lissa. You can come as you are if you prefer, it's irrelevant to me.' His super-cool gaze cruised down her body making her hot in all the wrong places. 'Just thought you might want a change of clothes.'

Then he stepped closer and she flinched involuntarily as memories of another man crowded in on her. Big, intimidating. Abusive. She'd thought she loved him once.

Shoving the sharp spasm away, she pushed at his chest. 'Personal space, *if* you don't mind.' He was warm, hard. Tempting to forget past fears and let her hand wander…to feel the beat of his heart against her palm. Heat shimmied up her arm and her own heart skipped a beat. She dropped her hand immediately, lifted her chin. 'I'm staying right here. On this boat,' she clarified quickly since they were still standing way too close. 'I should be here…in case something happens.'

'Something's going to happen all right if you don't get your butt into gear and move.'

She bristled at the commanding tone but he backed off. Still, she knew without a doubt, he meant what he said. And she hated to admit that he was right; what *would* she do if water started leaking through the light socket? Or worse. She'd never known such a downpour. The situation was much more dangerous than when she'd gone to bed. More dignified to acquiesce with whatever grace she could summon up.

'Fine, then,' she said crisply, over her shoulder as she turned and walked to her bedroom. '*You* stay here and keep an eye on things.'

'I intend to.' His voice boomed down the narrow passage.

Oh. Really? Obviously this superhero was immune to the dangers he'd so helpfully pointed out. Well, that suited her fine. She had enough problems without adding gorgeous male to the list.

She plucked the jeans and the T-shirt she'd worn today from the bottom of the bed, considered changing but decided against it. Stripping now with him only a few steps away would put her in a vulnerable situation, and she knew all too much about vulnerable situations.

'So, what, storms bounce off you, then?' she tossed back, grabbing basic toiletries and shoving them in a carry-all.

No reply from the other end of the boat but she could almost hear him: *I can look after myself.*

And she couldn't? She hurried back to the kitchen with her gear and came to a breathless stop a few steps away from him. Breathless because the impact of seeing him standing in her small living space all distant dark protector sucked her breath clean away. No, not all dark, she noted, because his eyes were cool, cool blue.

But they were still barriers. And he was still the intense brooding Blake she remembered from all those years ago. 'I'm not that helpless little thirteen-year-old any more.' Her cheeks stung with embarrassment. She hadn't meant to remind him.

A muscle tightened in his jaw and his gaze flickered over her, the merest glint of heat in the cool. 'I'm better off alone. That way I don't have to worry about you slipping and breaking a leg and drowning in the process.'

'I *do* know how to swim.' She thought vaguely that she'd like to sketch him now, with the lines of maturity settled around his mouth, around his eyes. Those sharp planes and angles of cheekbones and jaw—

He shook his head. 'You may not be helpless but I'm betting you're as stubborn as ever,' he muttered.

Stubborn? 'How would you know *how* I was?' She could do cool too. Iceberg-cool. 'I didn't exist to you.' She stepped away. Turned to the bunk beds against the wall. 'But yes, I'm very stubborn where my work's concerned. I have merchandise here I need to protect from the weather...should anything happen.'

'I'll take care of it.'

'Nice offer, but I don't want it to get wet.' She dragged a couple of plastic storage containers from beneath the lower bunk. 'If you really insist on this...evacuation...all of this has to be stored and brought to the house.'

'All?' He sounded doubtful. 'Do you really need it *all*?'

'Every last fabric swatch. My work depends on it. I'm an interior designer.' Unemployed interior designer at present, but he didn't need to know that.

'Come on, then, let me give you a hand.'

'Fine,' she clipped, packing the containers swiftly, anxious not to have him too close. His proximity was unnerving her; his musky warm scent was making her itch. 'If you could get those sketch pads.' She waved him away. 'There are plastic bags...'

It took them a few minutes to pack everything up.

'I'll bring the rest up to the house after we've got you settled.' He had to raise his voice above the rain drumming overhead.

Settled? Hardly. She straightened, a container beneath one arm, her carry-all over a shoulder. If he wanted to play Mr

Protector, so long as her stuff was safe from rain, she'd put up with it.

'Thanks.' Said grudgingly. She really did *not* want his assistance. Slipping into her rubber thong sandals by the back door, she slid the glass open and stepped onto the deck. A torrent of water slammed into her where it should be dry and she glanced up at the flapping canvas. She might not want his help, but she was forced to admit she needed it.

She stepped onto the jetty, Blake following behind her with a load of plastic-protected work. Her thongs slapped wetly as she made her way past the sapphire pool edged with moss-covered boulders, the palm-fringed undercover entertainment area to the wide glassed door.

Over the past couple of years she'd watched the beautiful house and its parade of beautiful people come and go. Now it was her turn to get a good look inside. It wouldn't be so bad to sleep in such luxury for a change, would it? And from a designer's point of view she couldn't wait to see the décor.

Didn't mean she had to like the arrangement but at least it was dry. She waited for him to come up alongside her and unlock the door, then followed him inside. He flicked a switch and light flooded the magnificent home.

She gazed up at the bright source of illumination. A myriad of tiny crystal spheres exploded from a central orb, splattering rainbows across the room.

Open-plan living gave it an airy atmosphere. The honeyed wood-panelled ceiling slanted high over two storeys, with a staircase against a feature wall in the same treacle tones leading to the upper rooms. White-tiled flooring merged with the white walls giving the impression of space. A black leather lounge with cushions in lime and tangerine tones was positioned against the exterior slate wall. The minimal furniture was teak and glass.

Stunning. But impersonal and maybe a little dated. It had been rented out for years to wealthy international jet-setters and lacked that lived-in ambience. A tingle of excitement lifted her. Maybe she'd ask if he wanted to redecorate...

They offloaded the stuff in one corner.

'I'll go back for the rest in a moment,' he said, already walking towards the stairs.

As he led her to the mezzanine floor she admired a wall of rich wooden patchwork. She did *not* admire the shape of his taut backside encased in those hip-hugging black jeans—she imagined a painting or feature of some sort in soothing blues on the wall instead.

She thought of all the times she'd looked at the house and never known Blake owned it. In fact, she hadn't thought about Blake in a while. But now...now it was as if those intervening years had never happened. Her feelings were as bright and strong as they'd been back then. And just as futile. But they zinged through her body and settled low in her abdomen at the prospect of dreaming about him again. They'd always been such...interesting dreams.

He indicated an expansive room with thick cream carpet and a mountain of quilt in striped olive green and black. The glossy black furniture was devoid of the usual knick-knacks. The window looked out onto the house next door and a view of the river. But not the houseboat.

Perhaps he'd chosen it intentionally, she thought as she walked past him and set her bag and clothing on a silk-covered boutique chair next to a chest of drawers. No way to spy on him. No way to drool over him and think lustful thoughts while she watched him work. Bare-chested, his skin gleaming, those rippling muscles—

'Shower's through there.' He spoke behind her. 'I haven't looked yet but I'm informed the pantry's been filled today so help yourself to breakfast in the morning.'

Breakfast. A sudden tension gripped her. She hoped Blake didn't decide to look in her pantry or her fridge because she hadn't stocked up for a week. She'd been skimping on meals, counting her last dollars. Breakfast was a luxury she'd managed without. And she *loved* breakfast.

Blake looked like a man with a large appetite. A breakfast-with-the-lot kind of appetite. In fact the way he was watching her, eyes kind of slumberous, lips slightly parted, he looked hungry right now.

Hungry enough to take a bite out of her... No. *Bad thought.* Her stomach turned an instant somersault and she licked suddenly dry lips before she realised she'd drawn his attention to them.

'I don't normally eat breakfast,' she lied. 'My cupboards are a bit Mother Hubbard at the moment.' *So don't bother looking.* 'Why don't you join me here in the morning?' *Why don't you stop staring and say something?*

'I was planning to walk into town and grab something there.'

Okay, so he didn't want to be anywhere near her. Humiliation vied with embarrassment and she was that attention-seeking thirteen-year old again. 'Suit yourself.' She huffed silently. Now she even sounded like a thirteen-year-old, all wounded pride and disgruntlement. She'd always acted differently around him. Why hadn't that changed?

To her chagrin, after all these years she was still allowing him to affect her. Helpless to stop all those teenage emotions exploding into her mind like big red paint splotches on a blank wall. As if time had wound backwards. As if he'd never left.

Disgusted with herself, she was already turning away when he touched her shoulder. A feather-light touch, barely there. So gentle. *So sensual.* She imagined suddenly, and with devastating clarity, how it might feel if her shoulder were bare and it were his lips rather than his hand. Heat blossomed where his palm rested and she jerked to a startled stop.

'But since we've a few matters to discuss...' he began in a neutral tone that belied the fact that his fingers sculpted over her shoulder were pressing ever so slightly into her flesh or that his thumb was creating tiny circles of friction on the back of her neck '...breakfast might be a good place to start.'

And for a few unguarded seconds she found herself relaxing into the sensations he was creating. The fresh scent of the soap he'd used to wash his hands. The shimmer of heat down her back from his body— *No.* She pulled away. 'All right.' Spoken coolly as she swung to face him. His hand slipped off her shoulder and she almost sighed at the loss. 'How do you like your eggs?'

'You're going to cook?'

He looked so surprised, she had to grin. 'I do know how these days.' And she had every intention of being up and dressed and *prepared* before he arrived.

He nodded without a glimmer of humour. 'Shall we say oh six hundred?'

'Make it seven.' She needed time to acquaint herself with the kitchen.

'Seven, then. I'll rescue the rest of your gear then take a look at the boat. Do you have anything I can use for repairs?'

'Try on the deck by the door. Under the tarp.'

He nodded. 'Goodnight, then.'

'Goodnight. And be careful.'

'I'm always careful.'

She watched him turn and walk away. Was he? *What about Janine Baker?* a little voice whispered. Janine had left town too and Lissa had never heard, nor asked, what had happened to her or her baby.

She was still watching when he turned back. 'And the eggs...? I like them hard.'

'That makes it easy, so do I.'

She had the distinct feeling neither of them were talking about eggs.

As soon as she heard the front door close she headed for a better view of the river. And Blake. She found it in the master bedroom. With the living-room lighting spilling onto the rain-swept patio, she watched him stride swiftly down the path. Past the pool. Along the jetty. A tall, impressive masculine figure, an image no less powerful than when he'd been standing outside her door as a possible intruder. And no less unsettling.

When he'd disappeared onto the deck, she turned and gazed at the room. The light from the hallway slanted onto the rumpled king-sized bed, the upper sheet twisted and hanging off one side. The imprint of his head on the pillow had her stomach fluttering with the kind of nervous excitement he'd always instilled in her whenever she'd thought of him.

She crushed a hand against her middle and ordered herself to settle down. He'd been sleeping in here. Or trying to. What had made him up and leave such comfort and seek out the houseboat in the middle of the night? Bad dreams? Or physical pain—she'd seen it behind his eyes, hard and brittle as if he'd been fighting it a while.

Or was he missing a special woman that he'd left behind in some foreign country?

She looked about for some hint. His open bag lay on the floor against a wall, clothes neatly stacked inside. A pile of sail-boat brochures were stacked on the dresser along with his passport and some loose change. She was so tempted to look at his passport and see where he'd been, but she couldn't bring herself to invade his privacy.

Instead, hardly aware of what she was doing, she moved to the bed and picked up his pillow, closed her eyes and breathed in. It smelled of sunshine with a subtle whiff of masculine scent that she'd come into close proximity with earlier. It had been a long time, but she remembered that smell. Blake. A moan started low in her stomach and rose up her throat—

'Everything okay here?'

Oh, God. Her heart jumped into her mouth. Oh, *no.* Her knees almost buckled from under her and her eyes snapped open though she'd rather they'd stayed shut. Then she could have imagined herself invisible instead of seeing Blake standing in the doorway, one arm on the doorjamb, head cocked to one side. His dark figure blocked the light from the hall. She had no idea what his expression was, or what he must be thinking, but it couldn't be good.

'Yep. Everything's fine.' Forcing a smile, she stepped away from the bed. 'I...ah...wanted to check the boat was still afloat.' She laughed; too bright, too high. 'Silly, I know...' *But you already have that opinion about me.* 'I'm...just grabbing an extra pillow on the way if that's okay... Was there something you wanted?'

And how dumb was she, how *reckless*, standing next to his bed in the semi-darkness in her mini nightgown and asking that question? Not that he noticed...or did he? He wore a bemused expression and she pressed her lips together before she got herself into even more trouble.

'My phone.' He turned on the light, regarded her a moment longer then switched his attention to the empty night stand and frowned. 'You haven't seen it, have you? I'm sure I left it here somewhere.'

She shook her head. 'Perhaps you knocked it onto the floor.'

'Or perhaps you did,' he pointed out. Faintly accusing.

Anxious to move this beyond-embarrassing situation right along and leave, she dropped the pillow on the bed and sank gratefully to her knees to hide her flaming cheeks.

'Is it there?'

'Um...'

'Do you need a hand?'

Oh, *yes, please.* The impact of those somewhat ambiguous words spoken in that low sexy drawl invoked an image she was better off not thinking about. 'Ah...' Her fingers closed over smooth plastic. 'Found it.'

Blake heard her muffled reply as he watched her silk-draped bottom wriggle backwards. She had it all right: the perfect backside. He tried, he really did, but he couldn't tear his eyes away. It had been a long time since he'd seen anything so…spectacular.

The last time he'd seen her she'd been a skinny thirteen and a blusher. Still was apparently. Her curtain of auburn hair obscured her face but he knew without a doubt that her cheeks matched it. She could be telling him the truth about the pillow and the boat but he seriously doubted it.

She was attracted to him.

Jared's little sister. Jared's very attractive, very sexy little sister.

She pushed up, held his phone at one end as if it were red hot.

'Thank you.'

'Sure.'

If she felt that zing when his fingers came into contact with hers, she didn't show it. She smoothed her hair behind her ears, straightened and met his gaze almost defiantly. Pink-cheeked and pretty.

Not words that normally came to his mind, but they suited Lissa. His chest cramped in an odd way. Sitting too long in the one position, he assured himself.

A scowl tightened his facial muscles and he studied his phone, pressed a couple of buttons. He didn't do pink and pretty and its association with hearts and flowers and ever afters. It wasn't for guys like him, always on the move. What was more, he didn't need it. *Way* too problematic.

Hot and fast and uncomplicated—*that* was what he needed. And by crikey, he thought, his lower body suddenly hard as rock, he needed it soon.

'Got someone special waiting for you to ring, huh?'

His head jerked up. 'You always did get straight to the point, didn't you? I need to make a few calls.' A plumber and an electrician for starters. But it could wait till morning.

'Your tools are worse than useless. I've secured the tarp over the main leak for now. Are you even aware of the state of the roofing?'

She looked away. 'I was going to get around to it.'

Yeah? When? 'I'll organise something for tomorrow.' He turned and walked to the door. A thought occurred to him and he turned back...and his mind went blank.

She was holding his pillow by one corner and staring at him. He imagined himself walking over there and taking it from her hands, leaning close and breathing in the scent of her neck. Feeling the silky heat of her flesh against his knuckles as he untied her sash and slid the dressing gown from her shoulders before laying her down and letting her help him forget why he'd come home.

But pink and pretty didn't deserve to be used in that way. *She* didn't deserve to be used in that way.

She arched a brow, waiting, and he realised that he'd been about to ask a question before he'd been blindsided. 'Are you working tomorrow?'

She hesitated, looking uncertain. 'No. Not tomorrow.'

She also sounded vague. 'Are you sure?' he prompted. 'You're not thinking of playing hooky, are you? Because—'

'Because you're here to take care of everything and not to worry my pretty little head over it?'

Right. He wouldn't have said it in quite that way but, yep, that pretty much summed it up.

She made a dismissive snort and didn't look the least bit impressed. She had that sulky pout going on again.

He didn't see the problem. Protection came naturally to him. Other women would be grateful for his assistance. And only too willing to show that gratitude. In any number of ways.

Not Melissa Sanderson apparently.

'Okay. Fine.' *Whatever you say.*

But there was something she *wasn't* saying, he could see

it in the way she evaded his eyes. He also remembered the almost hunted gaze from earlier and the way she'd pushed at him. 'I'll say goodnight, then,' he clipped. 'Oh, and if you're looking for a spare pillow, there are three other bedrooms to choose from.'

As he walked out into the stormy night he wondered whether she had, in fact, planned to sleep in his bed. The thought of that soft satiny skin on his sheets and that alluring feminine scent on his pillow smouldered through his bloodstream. Lengthening his stride, he distanced himself as quickly as possible.

CHAPTER THREE

BLAKE carried the rest of her decorating gear up to the house, then returned to see what he could do about the mess. He swapped the small container beneath the now free-flowing drip for a bucket and snatched up a newspaper from beside the couch to absorb the water on the floor.

As he spread it out he noticed an ad for a retail assistant's job in a beachwear shop circled in a red felt-tipped pen then crossed out with 'TOO LATE' scrawled beneath it and a sad face. Hadn't Lissa said she was an interior designer?

Was that why she wasn't working tomorrow? Because she didn't have a job? He glanced over to the final notice on the fridge door. Obviously she was in financial difficulty and just as obviously she hadn't told Jared because if he knew his old mate, no way would he have let this situation arise. No job and inadequate accommodation. *Dangerously* inadequate accommodation.

Bloody hell.

Blake had inherited a duty of care here. Not only because it came naturally to him but because Jared had been his closest mate, the brother he'd never had. As a young teenager, when neither of his parents cared whether he even came home at night, Jared had been there. Until his friend had taken on the heavy responsibility of parenting. It was no wonder he'd done such a good job with his sisters.

The rain continued to pelt down while he surveyed the

deck once more. Nope. Useless to try doing anything more until the storm blew out to sea. He went inside to ensure all the windows were closed, located the fuse box and turned the power off.

Then he stood on deck a moment, glaring at the house while water sluiced down his face and soaked down to his skin. He needed the chill factor. The fire in his groin, which had been smouldering since he'd first laid eyes on Lissa, had morphed into a raging inferno the instant he'd seen her nose buried in his pillow.

Hell, he needed more than wind and water to douse the flames. He needed a woman.

And now he was going to have to try and sleep up there after all, knowing one very attractive, very sexy woman was a few quick steps away down the hall.

The strip of golden sand was strewn with shells, driftwood and dead palm leaves where the rainforest met the sea. An azure sky, the air laden with the pungent smells of lush vegetation and decaying marine life. It should have been a tourist paradise.

Even in sleep, Blake knew it wasn't. Because the heavy pounding at the back of his skull was gunfire.

He'd been one of five clearance divers on the beach that day. It had been a routine training exercise. Until the jungle had exploded. Exposed and caught unprepared, they'd returned fire and made a run for it. But the newest member of the unit, Torque, had frozen.

No time to think. Blake dodging bullets as he retraced his steps. Grabbing and dragging the quivering kid back across the beach with him. Then more shots, searing the air and zinging past his head. Torque's last agonised cry as he fell against Blake, knocking him off balance. Rocks coming up to meet Blake as he fell. Then blackness…

* * *

Blake woke dry-mouthed, shaking, his heart hammering against his ribs. He was chilled to the bone, lathered in sweat, his skull reverberating as if he'd been struck from behind by Big Ben. It took a moment to draw breath, fight off the sheet, which had twisted around his legs.

He reached for the heavy-duty painkillers on the bedside table, swallowed them dry. The hospital doctor had ordered Blake to take them for at least another week. But he'd refused the sleeping pills even though he never slept more than a couple of hours at a time. If only the doc could prescribe him some magic potion to take away the nightmares.

He pushed upright and stared out of the window where the pre-dawn revealed a star-studded charcoal sky swept clear of last night's storm. Torque had been just a kid, full of fresh-faced ideals and too damn young to die.

Blake had been that young idealist too, once.

Unwilling to subject himself to further night horrors, he rose, pulled on a pair of shorts. He almost forgot about the boat—he glanced out of the window again to make sure the thing was still afloat, then headed downstairs. Past the bedroom where Lissa dreamed untroubled dreams.

Stopping in front of the living room's glass door, he slid it open to let the damp breeze cool his face. He could almost smell the nightmare's beach and the decaying marine life. The hot scent of freshly spilled blood.

He heard a shuffling noise behind him. His military-honed senses always on alert, he swung around, one fist partially raised.

Lissa. In the shadows. Eyes wide. Looking as fragile as glass in that tiny excuse for a nightdress. And shrinking away from him. Perfect. He'd terrified the life out of her twice in one night.

A wave of self-loathing washed over him. Gritting his teeth, he turned back to the window. 'What are you doing here?'

'I heard a cr— I heard a noise.'

He could hear the soft sound of bare feet as she crossed the floor and groaned inwardly, imagining those feet entwined with his.

'What are *you* doing here?'

He didn't answer. Just closed his eyes as the scent of her wafted towards him. Fresh, fragrant and untainted. She knew nothing of the atrocities committed beyond her protected little world. And he wanted to keep her that way. Safe.

Safe from him.

'Are you okay?' Quiet concern with a tinge of anxiety.

'Yes. Go on back to bed.'

'But you…'

Her hair, a drift of scent and silk, brushed his chin as she stepped in front of him. The feather touch of one small hand on his bare arm. 'I thought I heard… Are you sure you're okay?'

His eyes slid open. Wide eyes blinked up at him in the dimness. And those luscious lips… He could all but taste their sweetness on his own. She barely reached his shoulder. So tiny. His hands rose to hold her. To keep her away. To keep her safe. He could feel the firm muscles of her upper arms move beneath warm flesh.

Then he was sliding his hands up and over her shoulders, his thumbs grazing the petal-soft indentations just above her collarbones. He'd forgotten how smooth and silky a woman's skin felt. How different from his own.

His whole body flexed and burned and throbbed. So easy to lean down, seal his lips to hers and take and take and take until he forgot.

But he'd never forget. He could never be that casual young guy she remembered. The remnants of his dream still clung to him like a shroud. Contaminating her. Dropping his hands, he turned away from those beguiling eyes. 'Go away, Lissa, I don't want you here.'

He barely heard her leave and when he glanced over his

shoulder a moment later she was gone. Without another word. Relief mingled with bitter frustration. Damn it all, he didn't want to offend her. He waited a few moments then went back to his room and pulled on his joggers. A two hour run might rid himself of some of his tension.

The street lights still cast their pools of yellow, and after last night's turbulence the air's stillness seemed amplified as his feet pounded the pavement.

Lissa tossed and turned for the next couple of hours as the room slowly lightened. She'd left Blake's pillow right alone and taken a spare from another bedroom as he'd suggested. To prove that her story that she needed an extra wasn't a lie to get her out of an embarrassing situation. Not that he'd believed her for a second and she cringed at the memory. Why the heck had she bothered? Her pillow worries wouldn't even register on his horizon—not after seeing him downstairs in the darkness.

Hurting and alone and determined to stay that way. She'd heard him cry out. And for a moment she'd thought maybe she'd helped a little until he'd dropped his hands from her shoulders as if the touch of her skin had burned him. His curt dismissal had stung, especially when for a heart-trembling moment earlier she'd thought he was going to kiss her.

Which only proved she *still* had zero understanding when it came to men.

She would *not* take it personally. If she remembered anything about Blake at all, he'd have refused anyone's help. Except she hated seeing anyone hurting like that.

As soon as the boat was repaired she could be out of his house. Right away from him. Away from temptation.

Except for his claim that he owned the boat...

That wasn't a problem she could sort on her own so there was no use dwelling on it now. She threw back the sheet and rose. The storm had passed, leaving the sky a glorious violet-smeared orange. She opened the window to enjoy the bird's dawn chorus and early humidity.

Leaning on the sill, she looked out over the palatial homes and their moored million-dollar yachts and reflections on the river. A private helicopter circled further up the river then landed on its helipad.

She could hear a steady splash beyond the high concrete fence. Their next-door neighbour, Gilda, whom Lissa had met and spoken to a few times, was taking her regular early-morning dip in the pool.

Gilda Dimitriou was a well-known socialite, heavily involved in charitable works. Her husband, Stefan, was some bigwig in finance and they frequently entertained. Lissa was probably the only person within a hundred-kilometre radius without a high-flying job and a bulging bank account.

A fact that Blake Everett did not need to know. No one knew about her financial situation. Not even her family. Especially not Jared. She didn't want or need his help. Hadn't she spent the past year and a half proving that she could manage just fine in Mooloolaba on her own? Mostly.

Except that the interior design shop she'd worked for had gone out of business due to a dodgy accountant, leaving her with no income apart from a casual three-hour-per-week stint cleaning a couple of local offices. She'd had to put off the repairs out of financial necessity.

She'd hit a little bump in the road, that was all. She collected the clothes she'd brought with her. Determined not to see Blake until she'd showered and tamed her hair, no matter what dire circumstances and humiliations she was about to face, she headed for the en-suite.

And what an en-suite. It was as big as her entire houseboat. White tiles, gold taps, thick fluffy towels in marine colours of aqua and ultramarine. She breathed in their new and freshly laundered scent and switched on the shower.

After the boat's mere trickle, the water pressure was an

absolute luxury and she took her time, pondering her bump in the road. She still wanted to start her own business. It had been a bitter source of tension between her and Jared which had led to her moving here. She so badly wanted to prove she was capable.

Mooloolaba was a wealthy man's town on Queensland's Sunshine Coast. Plenty of people here would think nothing of paying exorbitant prices for a home makeover. She just needed to find them and convince them they needed her services.

Somehow.

For months now she'd taken cleaning jobs while scouring the papers and searching the Internet for the kind of work she wanted. Nothing. She'd had no response to her ads in the paper and on the net. The locals went for the services of the big, well-known, well-respected names. Lissa needed to come up with something different, something unique, get out there and make herself known.

Yes, she could drop Jared's name. His reputation for building refurbishments was well known around these parts. She wrenched off the taps and swiped the towel off the rail. No way. Absolutely out of the question. Because that would be admitting to Jared that he'd been right, that she couldn't do it on her own. And after walking out the way she had, she was too…ashamed.

So she'd have to settle for second best for a while longer. Which meant finding a full-time job—of any description. Which were few and far between. Back to square one.

And right now she had to face breakfast with a man she didn't know how to react to this morning.

CHAPTER FOUR

SHE had the toast buttered, coffee freshly brewed when Blake appeared in the kitchen on the stroke of seven. She just knew he'd be one of those super-punctual people. Always on time. Ruthlessly organised. Socks always paired and rolled together. How did he live with himself?

The only reason she was ahead this morning was because she'd been too wound up after their recent rendezvous in the living room to relax. She'd spent the time familiarising herself with the spectacular wood-panelled kitchen and every modern appliance known to man.

She'd psyched herself up for seeing him but the first glimpse still packed a punch as he walked to the kitchen table, leaving her breathless and feeling as if she'd run a cross-country marathon. He'd changed into a khaki T-shirt with some sort of blood and tar design all over the front but he still wore the same kind of snug-fitting jeans he'd had on last night.

He seemed more relaxed. His eyes weren't the haunted ones she'd glimpsed last night, even though they were still somewhat aloof, but, hey, this *was* Blake Everett and aloof was his trademark. Whatever his demons last night, he'd apparently shrugged them off. He'd showered and smelled as fresh as the new day.

Yes, a new day, she thought. Best to pretend last night never happened…

'Good morning.' Her smile was automatic, unlike his stern expression, as she lifted the coffee plunger and concentrated on pouring a mug without spilling it all over her hand. 'Coffee?'

He set a couple of those sailing brochures she'd seen on the table. 'Never touch the stuff. But thanks,' he added in what sounded like an afterthought.

His gravelly morning voice did strange things to her insides as he moved to the cupboard, pulled out an unopened box of Earl Grey tea. Real leaves, not the tea-bag kind. She watched him reach for a teapot on the bench, dump in a large fistful of leaves.

'Kettle's just boiled,' she said, wanting to be helpful and desperate to break the awkward silence that seemed to crowd in on them. She should have stayed right away last night. Stuck her head under the pillow or something.

'Not a morning person?' she said, briskly. He shot her a glance as he poured water into the pot. 'That's okay, I am. So that kind of balances it out, wouldn't you agree?'

He lifted a brow. 'I'm up at five a.m., rain or shine, how about you?'

Oh. She stared at him a moment. 'I've been known to drift home around that time.'

That earned her a look and she wished she'd kept her mouth shut. 'On weekends. Some weekends. As a matter of fact, if you're free, there's a party tonight down on the beach...' She trailed off as his jaw tightened. 'Maybe not.'

And not for her either. She studied him as she sipped her coffee. No, she wouldn't imagine he'd fit in with the party scene. She needed to forget her teenage crush, pull herself together and remember that he *wanted her boat*. 'How does the damage look this morning?'

'Haven't checked it out yet.' He poured his tea, already thick and black as molasses, and added two sugars, then took a seat opposite her at the table. 'After a closer inspection last night, I turned off the electricity, locked up and came back here.'

'Oh,' she murmured. 'I did wonder what you were doing in the liv—' Then bit her lip, wishing she'd never mentioned it.

'It needs major work,' he said, not looking up as he flicked through his brochures. 'Could take a while.'

She stifled a retort. It wasn't that bad, surely. It was just a ploy to keep her away and it wasn't going to work. After breakfast she was going to take a look for herself. She'd not gone down earlier because she'd thought he was there and didn't want the awkwardness of catching him asleep. After all, what if he slept naked?

She quashed the warmth that spun low in her belly and joined him at the table, pushing the plate of toast to the centre. 'You must have left eggs off your shopping list.'

'Toast's fine.' He reached for a slice, bit in with a crunch.

'You planning on going sailing while you're here?' she said, eyeing his reading material.

He didn't look up. 'Could be I'm planning on purchasing one.'

'But aren't you…in the navy?'

'Not any more.' He glanced up a moment, his eyes focused on middle distance. 'What do you reckon—sailing solo down the coast, stopping anywhere that takes your fancy. No time-tables, no schedules, no demands. Just you, drifting with the tides.'

'Sounds…' *lonely* '…magic. Is that what you're planning?'

'Could be.' He popped the rest of his toast in his mouth.

'You've given up navy life, then?'

'Reckon so.' He folded a corner of a page to mark it, then flipped the brochure shut, picked up his mug and leaned back. 'I'll ring a plumber this morning. And an electrician. Do you use anyone in particular?'

Obviously he didn't want to discuss the navy or his reasons

for leaving. 'Up till now, I've not needed anyone.' She nibbled the edge of her toast. 'Jared would know someone, but he's away.'

At the mention of her brother's name, Blake's demeanour brightened. 'So what's Jared doing these days?'

'He has his own refurbishing business in Surfers. He's on holiday overseas at the moment, with his family. They've been gone nearly two months.'

'Jared's married now?'

'Yes. He and Sophie have a three-year-old son. Isaac.'

'Good for him.'

His lips curved in one of those rare smiles she hadn't had the pleasure of looking at in ten years and her pulse skipped a few beats. At this rate she was going to need to see a cardiologist.

'You see them often?' he asked.

She refreshed her coffee, then nodded. 'Every couple of weeks and that's not counting birthdays and celebrations. I drive down to Surfers, though. A houseboat's no place for kids, it's too cramped and too dangerous and Crystal has two now.' She didn't tell him that after she'd walked away from her home, Jared made a point of not coming to Mooloolaba to see her unless specifically invited.

He regarded her a moment while he blew on his tea. 'When's he due back?'

'A couple of weeks.'

'I'll need his phone number. I'd like to catch up after all this time and I need to contact him about the boat.'

The boat. The way he said it. As if he'd retaken ownership already. 'No.' Her fingers tightened around her mug. 'You can't tell Jared about the boat.'

His brows rose. 'Why not? You pay rent.' He studied her coolly through those assessing blue eyes. 'Don't you?'

'Of course.' Except she'd missed last month's payment.

She'd assured Jared she'd have it by the end of the week. Stalling. Hoping another job would come up.

He'd be furious she'd not called him about the leak earlier but she'd been anxious to show him she was capable of organising things like repairs herself. And worse, Blake was going to tell him the boat was his, she just *knew* it. She had no idea who stood where legally but she couldn't let Blake take it from her. Wherever would she be then?

'Lissa.'

He brought her attention back to him, set his mug on the table. He met her eyes and she felt herself start to quiver. The soft way he'd just said her name… Oh, he made her weak. He'd always made her weak.

More like weak and stupid.

'What?' she demanded, knowing he wasn't going to say something she wanted to hear and determined not to fall for his husky low voice. His husky, low, *cajoling* voice.

'Forget about the boat and Jared for a moment. Tell me about you. Your place of employment, for instance.' The last words were silver-edged sharp as his gaze held hers.

She shrank back from the almost physical touch. Uh-oh, not cajoling, but worse. Much worse… 'I already told you. I'm an interior designer.'

'But you don't have a job at present, do you?'

Her stomach muscles clenched. She wanted to look away. Sweet heaven, she wanted to look away. Away from the man who'd starred in so many dreams for so many years. But these weren't the lover's eyes she remembered from those dreams. They were the eyes of a teacher demanding to see her homework and knowing she hadn't done it. No point denying it.

She placed her palms firmly on the table. 'Look, I'm having a few problems right now. Not that it's any of your business.'

'Make it my business, then,' he said, unoffended. 'I might be able to help.'

Help? Of all the people in the world, she didn't want Blake's help. She wanted him to go away and not ask difficult and embarrassing questions. But that wasn't going to happen. She smiled tightly. 'You know of a short-staffed interior design business round these parts?'

'Is that what you really want?'

Did he think her lazy? She'd been accused of burning the candle at both ends in the past and drew herself up straighter. 'Absolutely it is. I studied hard, have my diploma to show for it and I don't want to do anything else.'

He watched his mug as he twirled it on the table between them, then looked at her once more. 'So are you after employment or are you looking to branch out on your own?'

She took a deep, resigned breath. In a way it was a relief to talk to someone about it and he wasn't going to be around for long. He was nothing to her, she told herself. Nothing.

'Okay.' She studied her hands on the table to avoid looking at him. 'I haven't been able to get employment in any of the interior design shops here since the business I worked for went bust. So I have a low-paying part-time cleaning job, which doesn't allow for me to save anything like the money I'd need to start my own business.'

'Jared can't loan you the money?'

'I don't want Jared's help. Jared and I...we had a disagreement of sorts. I moved up here because I needed some space.'

'Space?'

'Space. Independence.' She lifted a shoulder. 'After I qualified, I worked at a design shop in Surfers for two years but I *know* I can do better than work for someone else. Jared told me not to rush it. We argued. I left. He didn't take it well.'

Blake studied her a moment; the intensity was unnerving. 'I'm sorry to hear that.'

She heard genuine regret in his voice and tried to shrug it off. 'We still get on okay.' Mostly. Except now she realised

Jared was right. She'd been in too much of a damn hurry. 'So I want to maybe freelance for a bit,' she continued, 'but people round here don't want to take a chance on a nobody.'

'You're not a nobody unless you think that way. Trust me, I know.'

Trust him? She met his eyes across the table—cool and calm and blue as a summer lake. Ah, so not only was he super-efficient and a protector hero, he was one of those super-positive, role-model motivational types as well.

But it was the underlying flame in those cool depths that turned her inside out and had her gripping the edge of the table and reminding her she was nowhere near ready to trust a man again. Not even Blake Everett. To have another man in her life, even as a friend, was a leap she wasn't sure she could make.

'I'll be fine. Something'll turn up.' Did she really believe that? Or did she just not want this man in particular to see her fail? 'How long are you here for?'

'I haven't decided yet. A few weeks, a couple months...'

Watching the play of emotions cross her gaze as she spoke it was obvious to Blake that she wanted him gone, as far away and as quickly as possible. But at the same time he saw the attraction shine out of those eyes and felt its burn all the way down his body.

He wasn't the only one confused, then. *Stick with what you know and leave the emotional minefield well alone.*

But emotion and attraction aside, it was obvious she needed some sort of financial assistance to get her up and running. It was just as obvious, a matter of pride for her, that she didn't want her brother's support. Which left Blake. And he owed Jared.

He guessed he wasn't going anywhere until something was sorted.

'Do you have a vision for this business, Lissa, should you set one up?'

'Do I ever.' She leaned forward, eyes alive with enthusiasm. 'In a nutshell: Beauty, Functionality and Innovation through Experience and Knowledge.'

She smiled with such glowing satisfaction that he just bet she'd been itching to give her spiel to anyone who'd listen.

More than a few thoughts flashed through his mind, none of them business, but he wiped out all distraction and focused on the here and now. His socialite mother's death had left him a wealthy man. He also owned investment properties here in his own right. Right now he was jaded and disillusioned. He needed a challenge, a distraction. Something new to light a fire in his belly.

Lissa Sanderson's vision promised all those things. He wanted to help her, not only because she was Jared's sister, but because she was young and vivacious and fuelled with the same energy he'd had at her age. At a fit and healthy thirty-two he was hardly an old man but he wanted that energy that had been lacking lately, that zest, back in his own life.

'Oh, and it must be eco-friendly,' she went on, 'working with rather than against the environment. And colour. Lots of colour. Bold...' She trailed off as she caught his eye and her cheeks grew rosy. 'I'm getting carried away.'

So was he. With her ideas, the way her voice and its passion for her work flowed over him. But more so with the woman. Her eyes. Her emotions clearly visible with that hint of the sea in their colour. Her hair, its vibrant auburn tint catching the morning sun, her creamy skin. He fisted his hands and rubbed his knuckles to try and curb the impulse to reach out.

He mentally shook his head, assured himself it was *purely sexual*. It was the perfectly natural response of a horny man to feminine sexuality. And far more comfortable than the alternative.

But she drew him in ways he couldn't explain. And he'd not felt that intriguing pull of desire for a woman in a long while.

He didn't *want* the alternative. Didn't want the complications that came with it. He didn't want to hurt her because of it. So…he'd need to make sure this…sexual tug…didn't clash with a possible temporary working relationship.

'I'm looking for somewhere to invest some money,' he said carefully. 'A business, perhaps.'

She went very still. He saw a tiny crease in her brow appear as she absorbed his suggestion. Her eyes took on a different shade. The way light changed when one moved from sandy shallows on some tropical shore to the deepest ocean dive.

'If you're thinking what I think you're thinking, forget it.' Her tone was cool. Very cool. Then she rose, took a few steps away. Distancing herself. 'I don't want or need your charity.'

'I'm not suggesting a handout,' he said, mildly. 'Charity was my mother's forte. I'm suggesting a partnership. I'll provide the start-up capital but you'll be the one slaving your guts out and responsible for the day-to-day running of the business.'

She turned. Her shoulders square, looking taller than her small stature, she hesitated before saying slowly, 'You mean you'd be…like a silent partner?'

'Exactly.'

'Why?'

'Because everyone deserves a chance and I like what I've seen so far.'

With a scowl, she crossed her arms, drawing his attention to the deep cleavage at the top of her emerald T-shirt. 'What do you mean—what you've seen?'

Uh-oh. Right word choice, wrong place to look while saying it. He lifted his eyes. 'I have to admit I flipped through some of your work last night before I brought the rest of your gear over.'

Lissa watched him from across the room, her sudden exuberance quickly dissipating. What would he know about interior design? He'd just eyed off her cleavage, what did that tell her? That he'd finance her business in return for sex?

No. She'd never stoop to that. Not to get herself out of difficulties, not for a chance at success. Not even for the chance of sleeping with Blake Everett. Rubbing her upper arms, she looked away. 'I'll find my own business partner, thanks.'

'It could take a while to find the right person and you don't have the luxury of time. Meanwhile you're not bringing in a reliable income and you're living on that pathetic excuse for a boat.'

He made sense. Damn it, why did he have to make so much sense?

'So how about taking me on until you find someone else?' he suggested. 'That special someone with financial backing *and* a flair for interior design who wants to take a more active role. When you find that suitable person we'll renegotiate.'

Little bubbles of cautious excitement fluttered as she leaned against the sink and studied the black slate floor. It would solve her immediate problems. She'd be able to afford the boat's repairs, pay off her debts, and maybe, just maybe, she could give herself a real chance at the career she so desperately wanted—

'There's one condition,' he said slowly.

The Catch, she thought, her heart sinking as she looked up and met his gaze. Wasn't there always a Catch?

Blake studied the wary eyes, the slight lift of her upper lip, the flared nostrils. Damned if she didn't expect him to suggest a wild, no-strings affair. And damned if he wasn't tempted. But this was his money he was putting on the line.

'I want to see how you work, so I'd like you to redecorate the living room here. It's been more than ten years and it's looking tired. I'll pay you, of course.'

Her posture straightened and a renewed spark lit her eyes. 'You'd let me have free rein?'

'Absolutely. And if we're both happy with how things progress—'

'But hang on, you said you're here temporarily.'

'Not a problem these days with email and the Internet.'

'So apart from the financial end, you'll keep out of it?'

'Unless you ask for my help, which I'm more than happy to give. Ah. One proviso, party girl. The business comes first. No coming home at dawn.' *Unless I'm coming home with you.* The thought popped into his head and he frowned. Where the hell had that come from?

She turned, reciprocated his frown with one of her own. 'Just because I was the Gold Coast's number one party fan, doesn't mean the legend continues here. I'm not eighteen any more, I've more important things on my mind. So I go to the occasional party—doesn't everyone?' Still watching him, she shook her head. 'No, I guess they don't.'

Damn right, they didn't. 'Say the word and I can have the money in an account this afternoon.'

She leaned back against the sink, fingers tense on the edge, and nodded slowly. Cautiously. 'Okay. But I don't want Jared to know. Not yet, anyway.'

'So we'll keep it between the two of us.' A sudden awareness—or was it wariness?—crept into her gaze and he knew she was thinking of the way he'd linked the two of them. 'It's just a business arrangement, Lissa. A temporary one until you find someone else.'

She nodded, blew out a breath. 'Okay, we have a deal.'

CHAPTER FIVE

'Oh...wow!' Lissa's whole being seemed to light up.

'We'll need it in writing,' Blake said, sharper than he intended, remembering the boat fiasco, which still needed discussing. After his father's betrayal, never again would he trust another as easily. No matter who it was. No matter how attracted he was.

'Of course.' Linking her fingers above her head, she laughed with surprising abandon, spinning a circle in the middle of the kitchen. 'I'll get right on it.'

She all but danced across the kitchen, reached up on tiptoe and flung her arms around his neck. 'Thank you.' Her breasts, firm and full and not constrained by a bra, grazed his torso, sending a spurt of lust straight to his groin.

Before he could respond in any way, she came to an abrupt halt. Her eyes widened, her cheeks coloured and she backed away fast. 'I...I'm going to go take a look at the room now and write up some ideas before you change your mind.' Then she turned and hurried from the room.

Lissa clutched her neck with both hands and willed the hot rush of heat to subside as she raced upstairs to her room. She'd got carried away and practically climbed up his chest. *Oh, God.* And he'd looked positively shocked. She went straight to the en-suite, splashed herself with cool water. She did *not* look at her reflection.

Sucking in calming breaths, she sat on her bed and took a few minutes to take stock and absorb the conversation. His generous offer. The offer that was conditional on whether or not he liked her work.

When she could breathe normally again, she walked downstairs to the living room and straight to her supplies stacked against one wall. To her relief, Blake was nowhere around.

She flipped her sketch pad open to a new page and sketched the room's layout. This was a tropical coastal town, so a beach or watery theme. Elegance. Simplicity. The furniture had to go. She glanced up. The exploding crystal orb of light stayed.

'Ideas?'

She heard Blake behind her but didn't turn. *No distractions.* 'Blues. Ocean theme. I'm thinking dull turquoise. It has both warm and cool undertones so it's compatible with almost any colour. It works well with charcoal—that slate wall's ideal. A lift with lime green or even red. Or if we go with a darker version of the turquoise, gold can look very dramatic, which could lend itself well to the honeyed wood...' She pulled out her big blue paint samples, chose two. She glanced over to him. 'Can you visualise your walls this shade, or is it too dark for you?'

'I'm leaving it up to your professional judgement.'

'But can you live with that colour?' She walked to the wall and held both samples up high, against the slate.

'I won't be here.'

Blake wasn't looking at the samples. He was looking at the strip of enticing flesh between her jeans and T-shirt. And all he could think of was how she'd felt pressed against him for those few seconds in the kitchen.

All he knew was he wanted that feeling again. He found himself standing behind her, breathing in the fragrance of her hair. His pulse drummed in his ears. 'The darker one. More full-toned.'

He heard her surprised intake of breath as he studied her

neat little fingernails against the colour card. When she didn't pull away, his hands closed around her waist, his fingers straddling the ridge between her T-shirt and smooth warm skin.

Her hands drifted down the wall; the colour cards fluttered to the floor. He turned her around slowly, looked down at her. 'I'm going to kiss you. God knows I shouldn't. You're Jared's little sister.'

Her eyes grew huge and glassy; her pupils seemed to swallow the green. 'I won't tell him if you don't,' she whispered.

He leaned nearer, felt her breath against his face. Felt the heat of her body against his chest. He pulled her closer. 'Ah, but I'm not going to lie to him, he's my mate. It's a matter of honour. But then I'm not feeling particularly honourable right now.' He dipped his head.

'After all this time...' she murmured against his mouth.

'After all this time...what?'

'Never mind.'

The breathless sound spilling from those luscious-looking lips, her fragrance shimmering on her skin, the sensation of two tight nipples pushing against the middle of his chest... No, he agreed silently, never mind...whatever it was.

His erection surged hotly against his jeans. Barely smothering an involuntary groan, he slid one hand to the small of her back and encouraged her body into closer alignment to ease the pressure down there.

It didn't. It only made him hotter and harder. And a whole lot hornier.

Denim shifted against denim as her legs moved against his. She stilled momentarily as the front of his jeans came into contact with her belly. Her eyes locked on his. Knowing, but not quite acknowledging. Not yet.

Then her fingertips crept up his chest, her arms slid around his neck. 'Unbelievable,' she murmured.

'Believe it,' he murmured back.

Lissa looked up into those liquid blue eyes framed with

thick dark lashes and wanted to drown there. She slid her fingers into his short military haircut and released a sigh that seemed to come from the depths of her soul.

Then, in a flash like a remnant of lightning from last night's storm, she hesitated. Did he *know* how she'd always felt about him? Was he about to take full advantage of that knowledge?

His erection butted against her as if in answer and, oh, how long had she wanted that? But, 'Wait…' She relinquished her hold and pushed at his chest. Reluctantly but firmly.

His brows lowered, his gaze turned bemused, those perfect, *ready* lips turned down at the corners, but he didn't quite let her go. His hands still rested on her waist. 'You okay?'

'I…yes.' Of course he didn't know.

But how well did she really know Blake? Did she believe the old gossip about him? She didn't know—she'd never had any personal contact with him beyond the casual 'hi and bye'.

She'd thought she'd known Todd. She'd trusted him with her heart, and with her body, and he'd abused that trust. In so many ways. The niggle turned to panic and flared bright and urgent within her. She started to pull out of his hold.

'Hang on, where are you going?' He tugged her back, his arms slid around her, steel bands holding her prisoner.

She fought down a sudden feeling of claustrophobia. 'I just remembered I need to…be somewhere.'

'No.' He released one arm to lift her chin with a finger so that she was looking up, up into his eyes. 'No,' he said again, softer this time, but no less demanding as he gripped her chin and dropped his mouth to hers.

Futile to fight it. The old thought flashed through her mind and hot panic geysered up her throat but as his lips moved over hers the bad drained away as quickly as it came.

She'd fought Todd when he'd made the same move on her over and over while she'd struggled and died inside, but here, beneath the heat of Blake's mouth, even within his uncompromising hold there was a whole world of difference.

Because she knew instinctively that she could pull away at any time.

Masculine dominance. Strength. Control. She'd come to fear them, but with Blake, here, now, it faded away like mist beneath a tropical sun. She felt none of that familiar trepidation, only a willingness to meet him equally, man to woman, and an urgent desire for more.

His stubble grazed her chin. Her legs trembled and she clutched at his T-shirt to keep from sliding to a puddle at his feet. She could feel the hard wall of his chest, leashed power humming just beneath his skin, the heavy thump of his heart against her fists.

This was nothing like a simple meeting of mouths. Nothing like it had been with any other man. Here, as his lips moved over hers, there was fire. The same fire, the same hot desire that burned brightly within her.

Until Todd had left her feeling inadequate as a lover, she'd never been a woman to shrink from her own desires, from taking what she needed from a man and giving in return. Celebrating her sexuality, absorbing her own pleasure, while ensuring she reciprocated in full measure. But she'd never felt the overwhelming emotional connection that suffused her whole being now, with Blake.

Her mouth parted only too willingly as he sought entry, his tongue dancing lightly over hers at first, then deeper, bolder, exploring the inside of her cheeks, her teeth. So easy to let emotion take command of her body as she absorbed the rich dark flavours he brought, the low growl she could hear deep in his throat, the feel of his fingers beneath her chin, against her neck. So simple to forget everything but this urgent, raw desire sweeping through her and give herself up to it.

Blake had never known that passion could be laced in such delicacy. His hands were unsteady as he tilted her head for better access to more of her sweetness, lifting them so he could glide his fingers through her silky hair and hold her close, where he wanted her. Where he needed her.

With her pale skin and clear translucent eyes she reminded him of a miniature porcelain doll. Easily broken. So he was careful to keep the fire that roared like an inferno through his blood contained.

Something had spooked her a moment ago, but now…now she clung to him, all lithe limbs and soft feminine curves. Her body melted against his, fitted with his as if she'd been made expressly for that purpose.

A rumble rose up his throat as he cruised his hands up over her shoulder blades, taking it slow, testing her response, testing his own. Then down her spine, all the way down so that he could tuck that spectacular bottom even closer against him.

But when his erection ground against her belly and she let out a sexy turned-on moan, all reason, all thought fled except the overwhelming desire to have her. His greedy hands raced up to skim the outer edges of her full round breasts. Taking their weight in his palms, he indulged in her warm, womanly shape.

Hunger. An insatiable hunger that demanded to be appeased. And need. Hot, acute, devastating need that rushed in with a torpedo's force to fill the void he'd learned to live with.

Dipping his head, he nuzzled a breast until he found its pebble-hard nipple. Heard her murmur, 'Oh…yes…'

He drew it into his mouth and suckled her through the soft jersey while his hands slipped beneath the hem of her T-shirt to feel her silky smooth belly against his palms. When he nipped at the erect little peak with his teeth, she gasped and arched against his mouth.

As if from a distance he heard a muffled sob as she cried out his name, sending white-hot shards arrowing straight to his throbbing groin. He shifted his attention to her other breast while he eased the T-shirt up over her ribcage, his thumbs already grazing the undersides of those perfect globes.

Then her hands pushed at his chest and through the roaring in his ears he heard the words, 'Blake...stop...'

Stop? It was enough to shake off the sexual fog that enshrouded them. He looked into those wide, passion-drenched eyes and knew she wanted it as bad as he. 'Okay, we'll take this somewhere more comfortable,' he murmured.

But when he ran a finger over the neck of her T-shirt, skirting the swell of her breast, she wrapped a restraining hand around his. 'No sexual favours...'

He frowned. 'Is that what you think this is? Repayment for my assistance?'

'I don't know, I...'

She thought so little of him? And suddenly he knew why. She believed the gossip. A bitter taste lodged in his throat. 'This is called sealing the deal with a kiss,' he muttered harshly, 'and you were enjoying it as much as me.'

'It wasn't *just* a kiss.'

Then his brain caught up with the rest of him. Her wavering, the hesitation. Her incredulous, 'After all this time.' Her reluctance to explain. Ah, hell.

She was a virgin.

And here he'd been well on the way to spreading those lovely tanned legs wide and taking her against the slate wall. For God's sake. She *should* think so little of him.

Gritting his teeth against his throbbing erection, he backed off. Carefully. Her virginal dreams no doubt included love and commitment. *Not* being taken against a damn wall. No way...

Lissa dragged in some much-needed air. Needed because he'd just kissed her as if the world were coming to an end and sucked her oxygen clean away. She felt as if she were waking from a dream just when it was getting to the interesting part.

Her sensitised nipples were begging for more of that attention he'd been paying them. Why had she stopped him? Calling a halt to the most exciting sexual experience of her life *and* with the man she'd most wanted to experience it with?

Because at this point in time she needed something more.

She didn't know Blake well enough for this *intensity*. But she knew of his reputation...

'This is going way too fast,' she said, still struggling to catch her breath. 'Right now I'm more interested in an income than...anything else. I can't risk any distractions getting in the way of that. So priority one: I need to focus on this room makeover. Okay?'

He didn't return her smile, possibly because she wasn't even sure she *had* smiled. Her tingling lips felt as if they belonged to someone else.

'Understood.' He shoved his hands in his jeans pockets. 'I'll organise for the arrangements to be detailed in writing immediately.' He spoke as though he were chewing on scrap metal and his brows lowered over eyes carefully blanked of all that emotion she'd seen only seconds ago. He backed away as if he couldn't wait to be gone.

'Great. The sooner, the better.' Her hand itched to reach out and touch his morning-stubbled jaw and tell him...what? That she'd changed her mind and wanted him to finish what he'd started and to hell with everything else?

'I know a solicitor.' His voice was as stiff as the painful looking bulge in his pants. 'I'll check whether she's still in the area and give her a call now.'

Chewing on her still-throbbing lips, she looked away quickly down to her hands in front of her. 'Right. Okay.'

He turned on his heel and left the room.

Lissa watched him go, her pulse still galloping from here

to eternity. She touched her mouth, still damp from Blake's. With him she was still that naïve girl who didn't know any better and who hadn't learned that she didn't choose wisely when it came to men.

Right now her career future was more important than getting intimately involved. If it went wrong between them she could lose this chance to makeover his room and any future financial backing.

And yet...he'd not taken her without care. He'd stopped when she'd asked. He'd considered Jared and spoken of honour. How many men spoke of honour, for goodness' sake? He was a decent guy. Those rumours had to be *wrong*.

Todd was the reason she didn't trust men's motives. His dark good looks had hidden an even darker side. The Toad had lied to her about his past and manipulated her feelings for him. A man of deceit and no morals. The opposite of Blake in every way that counted.

But she wouldn't think about how right and perfect Blake's body had felt against hers or the taste of his kiss...oh, no, she would *not*. That road led to certain heartbreak. Because he could be gone at any time.

She picked up her dropped paint samples. She was counting on Blake not telling Jared about the boat's problems or their agreed partnership until she gave the nod. She'd concentrate on his generous offer, pay for the repairs from the income she made and work her backside off to show she was worthy. To show him, and herself, and then her family that she could be the successful career woman she wanted to be.

First up, she'd impress him with her transformation of his living room. With renewed enthusiasm, she shimmied towards the wall with her paint samples and a swatch of gold-coloured fabrics.

Blake poked his head through the doorway catching her mid-shimmy.

'Can you be ready to leave in thirty minutes?' His gaze

drifted from her hips to linger on her breasts where her T-shirt still bore the damp circles from his mouth.

A flush crept up her neck. 'I'll be ready.'

Her reply finally drew his attention to her face. 'Great,' he said, and disappeared again.

Lissa glanced at her tell-all top and jeans. But not in these clothes.

Blake returned to the study, pleased with the ease with which he'd been able to organise the solicitor. Deanna Mayfield was an old school friend from Surfers who practised law in Mooloolaba. She was twice divorced and had been delighted to hear from him. She'd even juggled appointments to fit them in.

Next, he arranged for a plumber and an electrician to come in the afternoon, then searched the local area for men's clothing stores on his laptop.

It kept his mind occupied and therefore off Lissa and what had happened in the living room. That had been his intention, except that he could still taste her, could still smell her scent on his clothes.

He'd made her a business offer in one instant and kissed her to kingdom come in the next. Only he hadn't stopped at a kiss. He'd been so blind-sided it hadn't registered that she might be a virgin. How many twenty-three-year-old virgins were there these days?

Was she keeping it for Mr Right? Or was it because she hadn't she found a guy with enough power and vigour to light her fire? He preferred the latter. He was no woman's Mr Right and he'd already glimpsed the smouldering evidence in her eyes.

He drummed restless fingers on the desk. Trouble with virgins was they attached too much emotion to the sexual act and the last thing he needed was an emotional female who expected more. He had a gut feeling Lissa would be a woman who expected that 'more'.

She was Jared's sister. Getting physical with a mate's sister was one thing, but when said sister was a virgin? No way. No how. Out of bounds.

He needed to remember their agreement and maintain his focus on the goals they'd set and his hands off her body.

Her vivacious, voluptuous, *virginal* body.

His gaze flicked to the Titian-haired reclining nude in a Pre-Raphaelite original painting, titled 'Chastity', on the wall and wondered vaguely why his father hadn't tried to sell it. Had to be worth a quid.

Disturbed by the maidenly beauty and its similarity to a certain redhead, he averted his eyes and glared at the computer screen. Perhaps he and Deanna could have a drink later, catch up on old times.

He thought about the six-foot-tall blonde who'd won the Miss Sunshine Contest at seventeen when he'd been a gangly star-struck sixteen. Maybe he could suggest they...what?

On an oath, he shut down his computer. The thing was... the *mystery* was...he had a churn-in-the-gut feeling that no woman was going to take the edge off his need unless that woman was Lissa. The sooner he had the business plans drawn up and boat repaired, the better off it would—

Lissa's ear-piercing shriek from out back had him shoving out of his chair and bounding for the door.

Lissa stared in numb disbelief at the empty space where the houseboat had been only moments ago. 'Oh, my God, oh, my God.' She'd yelled until her vocal cords had given out and now she couldn't seem to raise her voice above a murmur. Her legs felt like spaghetti and every vital organ within her body was twisting and churning.

This was a mistake. A dream—a *nightmare*.

She heard the back door slide open. Heard a muttered series

of harsh four-letter expletives, then Blake's heavy footsteps sprinting along the path.

The steps slowed, stopped behind her. She didn't turn around. Her eyes were riveted on the swirling water, a gurgling liquidy sound and the rectangular shape disappearing beneath the surface. 'No!'

'Lissa.' Firm hands gripped her shoulders. 'It's going to be okay.'

She watched bubbles stream to the surface as her home sank deeper and blurred and felt herself start to shake uncontrollably. '*Going to be okay?* Going to be okay? My boat, my home, my whole life. Gone. And you're telling me it's *okay*?' Her hands flew to her face. 'Why didn't you tell me how bad it was? Why didn't you *insist* I pack up everything last night?'

She hated being told what to do so *why was she blaming another person for her mistakes?*

'We saved your all-important samples, that's—'

'My clothes!' she shrieked again. 'I've lost all my clothes!' Then they both stared in silence as a pale amorphous shape drifted up from the murky depths. Two small mounds popped onto the surface like mini desert islands.

'Well, maybe not all,' he murmured, and dropped to his knees, leaned down and plucked her buttercup bra out of the water.

'Oh…shut up! I hate you!' Vaguely, her mind registered that under normal circumstances the sight of his tanned long fingers on her most intimate of garments would have thrilled her, but right now all she felt was the burn of humiliation.

She snatched it out of his grasp. She couldn't look at him. Her eyes were stinging and deep inside she was very afraid she was coming apart and was disgusted with herself for that weakness. Why, of all people, did it have to be this particular man witnessing her defeat?

'Hey. I shouldn't have said that.' He turned her in his arms and held on tight. 'The Lissa I know is strong and resilient, she'll get through this.'

'How would you know *how* I am?' Her presence had barely registered on his personal radar. 'I was just a kid and you *didn't* know me.'

'Ah, but I did know you. You were one very determined, very single-minded kid.'

'Yeah, right.' He *meant* stubborn and spoiled. Indulged and irresponsible. Didn't this prove it? It had been her duty to look after Jared's boat and now...

But his reassurance was gruff against her ear when he said, 'The most important thing is you're safe.'

Safe? How was she safe when she had nowhere to live? Why hadn't she packed an overnighter, at least? She'd let him tell her what to do and now...now look at the mess she was in. She fought against him but it was like fighting against a warm rip tide.

'They're just things, Lissa. Everything can be replaced.'

'But they were *my* things,' she said, a single tear spilling down her cheek. 'Every stick of furniture, every knick-knack. My mother's bluebird of happiness brooch. They might mean nothing to anyone else but they meant something to me. I worked my backside off for it all, right down to the last scented candle. And before you ask, no, I don't have contents insurance.' Because she'd let it lapse two months ago due to lack of funds.

She felt him draw a deep breath but he didn't nag her. Instead, he held her against him and muttered soothing noises against her hair.

'You know something,' he said a moment later, 'I could fit all my worldly possessions in the back of a station wagon and I do okay.'

She looked up to see if he was joking. How did a person cram their life into the back of a car? Unbelievable. It wasn't normal. She let her forehead fall back onto his chest. 'You have this house. This *mansion*.'

'True.'

Closing her damp eyes, she gave up the fight and leaned into his musky warmth. And all she could think was if he hadn't been here, if he hadn't insisted she sleep in the house despite her vigorous objections, she might be at the bottom of the river now.

He drew back, still holding her upper arms. 'Guess we won't need the plumber's services after all.'

She opened her eyes and saw a dark splotch on his T-shirt where her waterlogged bra had been trapped between them. She lifted her gaze to his and, just for once, allowed herself the comfort of having someone to lean on. 'What happens now?'

CHAPTER SIX

AT HIS insistence, Blake made the necessary calls and organised to have the houseboat refloated and towed away. Lissa was grateful to Blake for his cool, calm and sensitive handling of the whole situation. A man to lean on in a crisis. It gave her time to regroup. Most of her artwork was gone. Photos, jewellery, books.

She sat on her bed and looked about her. She also needed time to absorb the fact that until she was making an income, this was her bedroom. She needed to pull herself together and decide that she could still be that independent woman she wanted to be but there was nothing wrong with accepting help now and then.

But did it have to be Blake's help?

She stared at herself in the full-length mirror on the bedroom wall. The boat disaster had briefly obliterated the excitement of the new business agreement she'd made…and that kiss. Oh, that kiss…and *more*. Her whole body burned and churned with the memory and she saw its instant effect in her reflection.

She shook it away and concentrated on applying make-up to mask her distress. She needed to forget that momentary indulgence. And to accept Blake's insistence that she remain in his home.

'Here?' She'd glared at Blake through narrowed eyes,

fighting it all the way. *Nuh-uh. Not going to happen. Not after that kiss and a half.*

'You have somewhere else in mind?' He'd waited for a response but she hadn't had a ready one. Not one of any sort.

Returning to Surfers and facing Jared with her failures was not an option after the regrettably immature way she'd walked out eighteen months ago. And in an hour she'd be signing papers and making Blake her business partner. She had to remain in Mooloolaba. Rental accommodation was high in Mooloolaba.

Sharing with a guy was something she'd sworn she'd never do again. Living with Todd had been the most harrowing time of her life. Not only the physical abuse but the lies and degradation. Made worse because she'd kept it a secret from those who would have helped her. She'd been so naïve, so ashamed, and, for a while, so broken.

'What are you afraid of, Lissa?'

She'd stared up at Blake and into those beautiful blue eyes. Blake wasn't Todd—was nothing like Todd—but she no longer trusted herself when it came to choosing the right kind of man.

'Nothing. Why would I be afraid? I'm certainly not afraid of you,' she'd told him when he'd scrutinised her face more closely. As if he knew her secret… *He couldn't know.* 'Thank you. I accept.'

She'd arranged to meet Blake in the living room before leaving for their rescheduled appointment with the solicitor. In her jeans and faded T-shirt. She groaned inwardly. The T-shirt with the two faintly creased circles on her chest. Now there'd have to be an additional clause with the expenses incurred to replace her belongings.

She descended the stairs at the arranged time. Blake had changed into smart casual clothes and her thoughts scattered like confetti. The white button-through shirt, open at the neck, enhanced his tanned skin and accentuated his broad shoulders and muscular frame, the trousers were slim-fitting, showcasing well-defined thighs and...

She swung her gaze to the wood-panelled wall, embarrassed at being caught checking out his masculine shape, and said the first thing that came to mind. 'Definitely the deeper turquoise. And a modern painting here that encapsulates the essence of Mooloolaba.'

'You're the expert.'

His eyes glinted and she knew that he knew what she was really thinking about. His hot, toned body against hers.

'Let's get the documentation over with first,' he said. 'Then we'll pay a visit to the bank and then you can go shopping.'

What could she say? She needed clothes. 'I'm... I'll pay you back. Every cent. You can take it off my fee when the room's done.'

'Don't worry about that now. But I've got some matters to attend to back here so I'll arrange to meet you at this address later.' He handed her a card and a key. 'It's a building I own. It was used as a prestige car showroom but it's been vacant a while. I was going to sell it, but it might be a good location for an interior design business. Maybe you could take a look, come up with some ideas and tell me what you think. Don't forget to key in the security code. Panel's on the right of the door.'

Her spirits lifted a little. 'Thanks.' She tucked the card in her bag.

'What about Jared?' He paused. 'I assume you're in contact while he's overseas. Shouldn't you let him know what's going on?'

Yes, but she had more than enough stress to deal with right now. Besides... 'I don't want to spoil his holiday.'

'He's your brother.'

She didn't look at him as she slung her bag over her shoulder but she felt a vague criticism aimed her way and shrugged off the prickly sensation. What was between her and her brother was none of Blake's business.

'I'll get around to it, okay?' Tonight. It would be morning in Milan then. She'd make herself comfortable and alone and phone him tonight. Maybe in a few hours she wouldn't be so likely to dissolve into tears in the retelling of it.

'What do you want to do about your belongings?' He sounded as if he was finding his way barefoot around broken glass.

'Of course I want to save what I can. But it's probably already ruined with salt and river grime and heaven only knows what else.' She bit her lip to stifle the sob. It made her want to throw herself into his arms and weep.

And perhaps, she thought, as she moved directly to the door without waiting, that was his intention.

Deanna Mayfield was just the sort of woman Lissa imagined Blake would find attractive. Any man would find attractive, actually. As tall as him, silver-blonde hair, trim figure. Even in her grey pin-striped business suit she exuded a sultry kind of glamour.

If you went for that kind of thing.

'Blake!' Her smile was pure toothpaste advertisement. She ushered them into her office. 'What a pleasant surprise to get your call.'

Ms Mayfield and smartly dressed Blake looked like an ideal couple as they reminisced about a past Lissa had no part in. Had they ever been lovers? She couldn't help thinking of the bad-boy reputation. Yep, she thought, Ms Mayfield would definitely go for bad boys.

Even when they eventually got down to business it was there. That…something. While Lissa sat within arm's reach feeling out of the loop, uninvolved and insignificant.

'We'll need a signature here.' Leaning over the desk,

Deanna flicked her hair and indicated with a passion-purple fingertip, then passed Blake her pen.

Lissa's lip curled, then she pressed a hand to the tender spot just beneath her breastbone while Blake signed and passed the pen back. With a smile. The knot was hunger, not jealousy. Good heavens, she couldn't begin to imagine how many women Blake would have been with over the years, no doubt all as glamorous as Miss Sunshine here.

Then Deanna smiled at Lissa as if suddenly remembering she was there and handed her the pen. 'Melissa. Your turn, sweetie.'

Sweetie. Condescending cow. Lissa stretched her lips into a smile over her clenched teeth as she took the pen and signed.

Blake dropped her at the Sunshine Plaza with her new personal debit card. The arrangement was that she should catch a cab to the address on the card he'd given her when she was done and they'd meet at five-thirty.

She headed into the mall to buy her blues away. She refused to get carried away however, knowing she needed to repay whatever she bought at a future date. Sticking to basics, she purchased underwear, toiletries, casual wear, a couple of business suits and skirts and a cream jacket...and, of course, the obligatory little short black dress.

She couldn't resist a tiny bottle of her favourite perfume and a couple of CDs—for therapeutic reasons. At an art shop she bought a new sketch pad, charcoals and pencils so that if she arrived at the premises before Blake she could keep busy. If she was busy she wouldn't think about the boat.

Fighting the dull pain that had been throbbing away at the back of his skull for the past couple of hours, Blake walked towards the shop. Standing across the road, he watched the lowering sun paint the upper half of the unique building a burnt orange. When he'd bought it, he'd been impressed right off with its central location—near other businesses but not overcrowded—and the interesting canted windows out front. Dodging a steady stream of slow-moving traffic, he let himself in with a takeaway meal, drinks and cutlery in a cardboard box.

The empty interior still blew him away. A gleaming expanse of polished floorboards flowed like a golden lake to cream walls on all sides. But the feature that really sold it for him was the main source of illumination. Two metal wheel-like structures a good couple of metres in diameter studded with down-lights and suspended at an oblique angle to each other and to the floor.

The building had a vaulted wooden ceiling and odd-shaped windows. Their topaz and sapphire glass threw out a rich palette of colours, glinting on the brass rail of the spiral staircase to one side, which led to a mezzanine level, which in turn floated above the rear third of the cavernous space.

It might have reminded him of a church except for the sound of a CD player crackling away with the unmistakeable voice of Robbie Williams from somewhere up those stairs.

With his box under one arm, he crossed the floor, appreciating the warm ambience. What better venue to launch an interior design business? With his mother's contacts and Lissa's obvious expertise, they couldn't lose.

But when he reached the top of the staircase he came to a silent halt.

Lissa was dancing, bare feet moving lightly in time with the song. A pad of some description lay open on the floor beside her. She'd been sketching…something. Didn't matter—he didn't even cast his eyes in the pad's direction. It was the woman he wanted to feast his eyes on.

The day's last vermilion beams lasered through the only upstairs window high above them, turning her magnificent crown of hair to flame, painting her limbs gold and leaving the shadowed spaces a dusky purple. He stood, transfixed in the stairwell's dimness. Held his breath, though he doubted he had any breath left in him to hold.

She'd changed into a loose white top that dipped low at the front. Beneath it she wore short white shorts leaving her legs bare.

Those feet moved fast and light, as if she were dancing on air, but her arms moved above her in a graceful arc, her gaze wholly focused at some point in the middle distance, her lips turned up slightly at the corners as if delighting in the moment.

It was like watching an angel.

Would she wear that same expression if he were lying beneath her? Would she make love with that wholly focused gaze and delight?

He shook his head to clear the lusty thoughts. Angels were supposed to be pure asexual beings, weren't they? And as far as he knew, they didn't make love. *Virginal.* But he could have watched for an eternity, absorbed in the beauty of the moment—and her—but she turned and saw him and that golden moment was gone.

For a breathless heartbeat she watched him with those wide clear eyes. Then she blinked as if coming out of a trance and slowly lowered her arms. Perspiration dewed her skin and her breathing was elevated, drawing his attention to her breasts as they rose and fell. He couldn't look away.

'Hi.' He kept his voice casual, breaking the sudden tension.

She lifted a self-conscious shoulder and colour rose up her neck. 'Hi.' Bending so that her hair curtained her face, she flipped the pad shut, creating a draught across the floor, and he caught the fragrance of some exotic perfume she'd not been wearing earlier today. It reminded him of midnight madness on a moonlit beach.

'I found an old CD player someone left behind.' She moved

to it, squatted down and lowered the volume. 'Have you been standing there long?'

'Not long.' Not long enough. Too long.

'Dancing's my stress reliever of choice. And chocolate, of course.' She helped herself to a four-square row from the half-eaten block beside the player. 'I guess I got carried away.'

'You don't share?'

'Sure, sorry.' She grabbed the bar, held it out. 'Help yourself.'

'Not the chocolate.' He gestured towards the pad. 'Your art or whatever you were sketching there.'

'Ideas for your living room. But you don't get to see them until I'm done.'

With the tip of her tongue, she licked a small fleck of chocolate from the corner of her mouth. He watched her, wishing he could've been the one to sample that sweet taste on her mouth. Then she wiped the spot with a finger for good measure and said, 'What have you got there?'

He'd forgotten all about the box. He withdrew the aromatic bag, held it up. 'I thought you might be hungry but I see you're already well supplied.'

She shook her head. 'Chocolate doesn't count. I'm starving. And that, whatever it is, smells delicious. Let me guess.' Closing her eyes, she inhaled slowly. 'Mmm...Indian.'

'Hope you like butter chicken. It's full of calories and comes with jasmine rice and assorted delights.'

'Ooh, yes. Hand it over.'

She reached for it but he lifted it higher. 'Not quite yet.'

She did the pout, her hands on her hips, but a glimmer of a smile teased the edges of her mouth. 'Hey, that's just mean.'

'First, answer a question for me. Earlier today you said you hated me. Is that still true?'

'I... No.' The tiny smile vanished and she frowned. 'Did I say that? I don't remember saying that. Of course I don't hate you.'

'Good. I don't hate you either.'

'Even though I've been such an idiot?'

'You're n—'

'But I am. I hold myself responsible for the mess I'm in and...and the trouble I've caused you.'

'And now we'll move on.' He mentally kicked himself for bringing up this morning's disaster and wiping away her smile just because he wanted some sort of petty reassurance. What the hell was wrong with him?

'That's a relief, since we just signed an agreement to work together, but can we have the rest of this conversation *after* we've eaten?'

He moved closer to better catch her scent. 'I've been thinking about you.'

'You mean that kiss.' She shrugged and turned away, refusing to play his game of grab-the-bag, but he saw her fingers tremble slightly as she popped the last piece of chocolate in her mouth.

'Ah...that kiss,' he said, slowly, and watched her cheeks pinken. 'Since you've brought it up...'

'*I* didn't, *you* did.' She dropped to her knees and busied those small hands putting her art purchases in a pile. 'I've had more important matters on my mind, actually.'

'So have I.' He set the food and the box holding the rest of the stuff on the floor, then shook out a rug he'd found in the boot of the rental and spread it out. 'Fact is, you're right in there with all the other stuff that's going on.'

She set the containers out on the rug and began removing the lids. 'I'm sorry if that bothers you.'

It did. More than she could possibly know. He watched the way her auburn hair swung down in an arc, hiding her face from view. 'I'll manage.'

'Of course you will, you're very capable. What is it you do again?'

Now her eyes flicked up to his. They were full of questions he wasn't going to answer. Not to anybody. The headache burgeoning behind his eyes intensified. 'I was a clearance diver. Like I told you, I've resigned from the navy.' *End of story.*

She blinked. 'O-kay...' When he didn't elaborate she glanced at the window. 'It's going to be dark soon. The lighting up here doesn't seem to be working.'

He welcomed the encroaching night and a change of topic. He wasn't going to spill his guts to Lissa Sanderson. Knowing her family background as she did, she'd be the kind of woman who'd want to try to nourish his soul.

If he still had a soul, that was.

'Lucky I brought these, then,' he said, pulling out a box of tea lights. He set half a dozen along the balustrade.

'You think of everything, don't you?' she murmured.

'It's my practical streak.' He shot her a quick glance as he lit them. 'I wasn't sure if the power company would make it here to switch on the electricity in time.'

He lowered himself to a corner of the rug on the other side of the feast and passed her some plastic cutlery and a plate from the box. She piled up her plate as if she hadn't eaten a square meal in a week.

'So, what do you think of the building?' He spooned some rice onto his plate.

'It's gorgeous,' she said around a mouthful of chicken. 'Absolutely gorgeous. Just what we need.'

He popped the cork on the champagne bottle, poured it. 'Have you had a chance to decide how you want to set it up?'

'Yes. I'll take you downstairs and show you after.'

He handed her a foaming glass, raised his own. 'A toast to our new partnership.'

'To success.' She clinked her glass to his.

To us, Lissa wanted to say. But despite the candles' soft glow caressing his face with bronze fingers and casting shadows in the violet spaces between them and the love song's words on the tinny player, this wasn't supposed to be a romantic dinner.

And she'd had to go and mention that kiss.

Obviously he'd not been thinking about it at all. Just because he'd said he'd been thinking about her, didn't mean he'd been thinking about her in any *romantic* sense. He probably had loads of women who'd been waiting ten years just for his call. Naturally he'd think about her, and it wouldn't be good.

She'd just managed to lose all her belongings and the boat he called his. He'd inherited a house-mate he hadn't asked for. And that wasn't all. He'd had no intention of being involved in a business, let alone an interior design one. He'd rather have his luxury sail boat. Was it any wonder he'd been thinking about her?

'Wine not to your taste?'

His voice dragged her back to the present and their surroundings. 'Yes, it's lovely. Thank you.' And so it should be, at the price she knew it sold for. French, too, always her favourite. She took a sip and said, 'So, the navy must pay you *very* well.'

He shrugged. 'I do okay.'

'Just okay?' Clearly he didn't want to talk about any aspect of his working life—his *previous* working life—or how they happened to be drinking one of the most expensive celebratory champagnes available.

'I live in military accommodation when I'm not at sea. I've never had a mortgage so I've put my money into buying property. This building for example.' He forked up a morsel of meat, but didn't put it in his mouth. 'If you're wondering whether I am, in fact, a secret international drug lord, maybe I should tell you my mother also left me a sizeable inheritance.' His expression betrayed nothing of his emotions regarding the loss of his mother.

Lissa remembered the car accident that had claimed Rochelle Everett's life and brought Blake home that last time. She'd been a popular social celebrity and famous for her charitable work from Surfers all the way up to the Sunshine Coast.

'I was sorry to hear about your mother, Blake. She did so much good for the community.'

He studied the meat on his fork. 'Can't deny that.' Then he jammed it in his mouth, chewed a moment and washed it down with a long, slow swallow of champagne.

Lissa felt the wall go up so hard, so fast, it made her head spin. Impenetrable. Insurmountable. What made a man so unwilling to talk about himself? Every aspect, every topic she broached, every time she tried to get him to open up, he stopped her cold. And it wasn't only pain she saw in his eyes, there was bitterness too.

She'd never known her mother, who'd died when Lissa was born. She'd also discovered a few years ago that she was the result of her mother's affair with an itinerant artist. The man she'd known as her father was dead and good riddance. But she couldn't begin to imagine the pain of losing Jared, who'd been both a mother and father to her in her formative years, or Crystal, her older sister.

But Blake's mother had been a *good* person, a caring person who'd worked tirelessly for charity and the community. What was it with him?

So she spent the rest of the meal covering easy neutral and safe topics, like her family. She told him how Jared had met Sophie when she'd emailed her not-so-secret diary to him on her first day as his PA and he laughed the bubbles off the top of his champagne. Then she regaled him with entertaining stories about her nieces and nephews.

He opened up enough to reminisce about his surfing days with her brother. She didn't ask him about his work or what he intended doing now or his family again.

When they'd finished the meal, Lissa switched off the CD player, stacked the plates and Blake packed everything back, standing the half-finished bubbly in one corner of the carton.

Finally out of safe conversational topics, Lissa waited for Blake to speak or fill the void with...anything. He looked at her for a long, hushed, tension-packed moment, his eyes glinting in the candle's seductive glow.

Anticipation swarmed through her body, her pulse picked up and her breathing quickened. She swore she could see the sexual sparks dancing between them on the candle-light.

But Blake didn't kiss her. He wasn't seduced or persuaded by those sparks. Instead, he rose, walked the couple of steps to the balustrade and blew out the candles, leaving only the light filtering up from downstairs. Back-lit, he was all stern lines and sharp angles and shadows. *Who are you really, Blake Everett? What's made you this way?*

Then he bent down, picked up his box and said, 'I think it's about time you filled me in on your plans for this place.'

CHAPTER SEVEN

LEAVING Lissa to follow, Blake blew out a strangled breath as he descended the stairs. A beautiful woman, a *willing* woman, champagne and candles. He could have had her. Right there on the floor, he could have given into the temptation that had kept him hard as granite all evening and most of the day.

He could have stripped away her clothes and watched her body bloom beneath his hands. He could have slid inside her, watched her eyes darken in surprise then pleasure. And he was walking away.

He shook his head. Some other man would have to introduce Lissa to the joys of sex because she was strictly out of bounds to him. And the pain in his skull was intensifying by the minute. Strobes of light impeded his vision, nausea rose in ever-increasing waves. The alcohol hadn't helped. He shoved the discomfort away. *Never allow another to witness your vulnerabilities.* He'd lived by that personal mantra all his life and he wasn't changing now.

On his arrival earlier, he'd had the unnerving feeling she was looking right into him when she'd caught him watching her at the top of the stairs. He hadn't enjoyed the sensation one bit.

Nor had he intended a seduction scene as such. One always celebrated a new venture with champagne. And the candles… He really *had* expected the power to be off.

Beneath the twin circles of light, he slowed to allow her to catch up. The empty building echoed with the sound of footsteps on wood as they crossed the polished boards.

A big hollow space, waiting to be filled. Kind of like where he was in his life right now. A place full of endless possibilities. He stared past the lights' glare to the darkened ceiling. Darkness into light.

He swiped a frustrated hand over his hair. Today had been one hell of a day and he wasn't going to end it by making an even bigger mistake with Lissa. A mistake that could cost them this partnership, and he knew she couldn't afford for that to happen.

She walked up and stood beside him, her shoulder brushing his arm, and said, 'Right, where shall we start...?'

He liked her ideas, suggested a few of his own. Her vision for the premises was well thought through considering she'd seen it for the first time this afternoon, the energy running through her commentary boundless. She pointed out a proposed office area, another space where clients could wait in comfort and browse catalogues. Areas for displays of soft furnishings and colour swatches, wallpaper, shelves to display interesting and unusual glassware or pottery. Another where clients could play with mock-up designs on touch-screen computers.

Eventually Lissa had said all there was to say. She looked to Blake for his response to her suggestion that she hang some of her own artwork on the walls. She'd saved a couple of her favourite pieces from a watery grave and she could create more.

He only nodded and she couldn't tell what he was thinking.

'If it's all right with you, I could set up at home in one of the spare rooms so it doesn't interfere with anything you might want to do,' she said.

'No problem. I don't have any plans for entertaining. Besides, I've never watched an artist at work.'

The thought of him watching unsettled her and she rubbed her arms in the cool swirl of air. 'Oh, I don't know about that.' A half-laugh trickled out. 'I've never worked with an audience.'

But when she looked at him her smile faded. His eyes. Haunting, hurting. Hungry. A well of conflicting emotions churned like a choppy sea behind that carefully neutral stare. A stare that defied anyone to try and find a way through.

She wanted to see the pain gone. She wanted to be the one to make it go. Right now she didn't care that she'd warned herself to keep away, that the business came first, that she didn't want her heart broken. She rested her hands on his crossed forearms and looked up at him.

She wasn't going to let their difference in height intimidate her. Rising on tiptoe, she reached behind his head and pulled it down towards her, keeping her hands slow and light, craving his taste again.

She felt his tightly crossed arms loosen, his body give as he leaned closer. So close. The scent of his skin surrounded her, his quickened breathing feathered over her mouth.

And then his lips brushed hers and her pulse went wild. How long had it been since she'd been brave enough to invite any kind of sexual contact, let alone initiate it? She crept her fingers between his forearms so that she could open them wide and fit herself against that broad hard chest—

He muttered something against her mouth that sounded like something a sailor would say. She felt the stiffness in his neck, resisting her, pulling back. Pulling away.

He uncrossed his arms all the way. Not to wrap them around her but to let them hang at his sides, leaving her own hands to drift down, useless.

'Lissa.' He looked down at her, the heat she'd felt emanating from him banished somewhere behind that shuttered gaze. 'I phoned Jared this afternoon.'

Pardon? 'You phoned Jared?' It took her a moment to gather her wits, pull her scattered self together and absorb what he'd said. Another before the feeling of betrayal slid cold and slick between her ribs. What had happened to keeping it between them? *Our little secret.*

'You made an agreement with me and you broke it.' The intoxicating moment fled and she clenched her fists against her stomach to stop the feeling of nausea welling up there. 'What did you do—scroll through my address book behind my back?'

'I looked up Crystal and Ian's phone number. Ian remembered who I was and gave it to me. I—'

'No.' She couldn't look at him. 'You had no right.'

'Wrong. It was the responsible thing to do. The only thing to do.'

'No.' She jabbed a finger at her chest. 'What I tell Jared is *my* business.'

'What, you'd have him drop by on his way home from vacation and find no boat? No Lissa? No way of knowing where you were?'

She shook her head. 'He'd never drop in without phoning ahead. It's called *communication.*'

'You weren't doing a very good job of communicating with him, then, were you?'

'What about you? Did you *communicate* with me about this first?'

'You were shopping.'

She lifted her head and glared at him. 'So?'

'I didn't want to have this conversation with you over the phone.'

'I told you I was going to let him know.'

'When? He loves you and you left him out of the loop.'

She knew, and it stopped her in her tracks. Worse, it had

taken Blake to point it out. 'That still doesn't give you the right to go over my head or mess with my affairs.'

What exactly had he told Jared? Had the two of them discussed her as if she didn't have a voice—or a brain? It made her want to slap something. Or someone.

'So you had a chat about Lissa's lapsed insurance too, then? The boat's state of disrepair? *Did you tell him you own it?*'

She stopped because she'd run out of breath. He wasn't attempting to deny her accusations. He was waiting for her to finish her little tirade. Calmly. Rationally. Only a tic in his jaw betrayed him.

'The boat's gone,' he said coolly. 'I've decided there's no point telling him my father sold it twice over. I assume Jared has insurance to cover it. He can make his own decisions about whether or not to replace it.'

Oh. 'That's very—'

'I told him what happened,' he continued, in the same unhurried voice. 'And that you were safe and unharmed and with me.'

With me. Why did those words claw so at her belly? She tightened her stomach muscles against the odd sensation and said, 'Nothing about our business arrangement?'

One eyebrow rose. 'You and I have an agreement.'

She nodded. She felt small. *Really* small. She'd jumped in feet first without thinking, without seeking clarification.

He went on, 'But it doesn't mean you keep him in the dark about it for much longer.'

What about that kiss? Did he intend not keeping him in the dark about that too? Oh, she did *so* not want to think about him talking guy talk with Jared about that. She comforted herself with the knowledge that they were mates, she was Jared's sister and Blake wasn't likely to spill that piece of information to her brother. Still, guys were guys…

And to think she'd been tempted to kiss him again. *Only to make him feel better.*

And he'd wanted to kiss her, it had been as obvious as the horn on a rhinoceros. And then at the last second he'd suddenly remembered he'd phoned Jared? He'd have known she'd react to that. It was almost as if he'd been looking for a reason, any reason at all, not to give in to that sexual hum between them.

She rubbed her arms to ward off a sudden chill. She should be relieved he'd put a stop to it. After all, she'd told him only hours ago that they were moving too fast.

'Okay.' She worked hard to keep her voice reasonable when what she wanted to do was yell why did he have to be so remote? As if he'd flicked a damn switch. 'But I wish you'd told me before you rushed into it. I'd intended phoning him this evening.'

'You still can.' His disbelieving look negated the barely there nod, making her feel like a kid again, and then he was walking away, cutting their conversation short with, 'It's late. Where's your gear?'

They didn't speak as they piled everything into his rented SUV. On the short drive home she pressed her lips together tight to stop the words she wanted to say spilling out: Frustratingly Infuriatingly Complicated Gorgeous Man.

When he pulled into the kerb outside the house, she glared straight ahead. 'I've changed my mind,' she murmured. 'I think I hate you after all.'

'I'll try to take it in my stride.'

They unloaded the car, both avoiding the other. When it was done, he muttered something about checking his emails and she saw him heading to a room off the living area that looked like a study. Or a cave. And he was damn well going to shut himself in there.

'Hang on.'

When he didn't stop, she caught up, planted herself in front of him, then waited until he looked down and at least acknowledged her. 'If you don't want to kiss me, you don't need to fake some spur-of-the-moment excuse to push me away. I'm a big girl these days, I can cope.'

He stood unmoving for a few unsteady heartbeats. 'Be very careful what you say to me right now, Lissa.' His husky warning sounded more like a promise than a threat.

But his non-committal expression just plain got to her. Did he have to be so…lone wolf? It made her want to push and prod until she got a reaction. Any reaction. She wanted to understand the demons she saw in his eyes in an unguarded moment. She wanted to understand *why*.

She pushed harder. 'I can handle rejection, I can handle disappointments. I can handle y…' She trailed off at his unforgiving stare, realising she'd let her mouth run roughshod over her thoughts, and took a step back, away from the intensity battering her.

His nostrils flared, his jaw clenched and something deeper than indigo flickered hotly in the depths of his eyes. He stepped forward, crowding in on her. Now she saw gold flecks among the blue in his gaze. Alive, like a flame. Raw and hot and primitive. For a brief moment he looked like a stranger—or that dangerous lone wolf—and instinctively she took another step back.

'You think you can handle me?' His hands shot out and his fingers curled around her upper arms, his thighs bumping hers as he walked her backwards with him until her spine came up against the wall. His unrelenting gaze didn't waver from hers.

He dragged her against him and kissed her. Hard. No time to react as his body flexed against hers, unyielding and unforgiving while his hands fisted tightly in her hair.

Then, before she knew it, he lifted his head to mutter against her shocked lips, 'You're not ready for what I'd like to do to you.'

The images his harsh words invoked sent a thrill pulsing through her. It throbbed low and heavy between her legs.

He untangled his hands from her hair and backed off. Without the support of his body, she slumped against the wall, dazed and dizzy and not a little delirious.

She knew her eyes were too wide, her breath too choppy, her limbs too trembly. She'd blown it, she could tell, and she saw a muscle twitch in his left jaw, felt him grow distant as he watched her through half-lidded eyes.

'And what would that be, that you'd like to do that I'm not ready for?'

His Adam's apple bobbed, his hands fisted at his sides and she swore the air vibrated with shared images... Blake pushing her back against the wall, tearing away her clothes with impatient fingers until she stood naked and trembling with need. Using his hands and mouth and tongue to bring pleasure to every square centimetre of quivering flesh, then ploughing into her where she stood...

Dull colour sprinted high along his cheekbones as if he'd been having the same thought. 'That'd be a mistake.'

She licked lips gone dry. 'How do you know it would?'

He shook his head but she could see she'd put a dent in that composure. 'I suggest you go upstairs and get some sleep.' Turning on his heel, he walked away.

'The night is young,' she called to his retreating back with a brightness she didn't feel. She watched him walk to his cave, his shoulders tense, his strides long and swift. 'I think I'll go to that party after all.' She said it loud enough for him to hear as he reached the door. He hesitated before closing it behind him with a firm click.

She sighed, a weird cocktail of frustration and satisfaction simmering through her. She'd had no intention of going anywhere but he didn't need to know that.

Forget the way he'd stalked off, she'd got to him. Rattled his cage. Woken the primitive man beneath the civilised exterior. A quiver of excitement jagged down her spine. Was she really ready for that?

But she wasn't the only one with something to fear, something to hide. And what would stop a man like Blake from acting on their obvious attraction?

His own code of honour. His integrity. She'd seen it in action. More than once. Her fingers tightened into fists. Damn the gossip-mongers. He didn't deserve to be talked about that way.

But the man clearly didn't do emotion. Never had. And she'd never understood how he and Jared had got along so well. Back then she'd been too young to question it, but not too young to imagine herself offering him solace any way she knew how.

There was pain too, recent and raw in his shadowed eyes. And he was alone here with no support base. She couldn't begin to understand how someone dealt with that. He could try and block her out but she was going to reach him eventually. No one should be an island.

Someone was playing the harmonica. Blake pressed the heels of his palms to his eyeballs as the familiar childhood sound drifted over the pool's still blue water and through the open window.

Tipped back as far as the recliner would go, he lay in the study's darkness while a bevy of hammers battered away at the back of his skull. Darth Vader and Luke were fighting their all-time classic laser battle inside his eyeballs. The nausea was still at the high-tide mark.

Had Lissa gone partying? Probably, after that scene against the wall. He'd had to get rid of her—it was that or lose his pride. Throwing up at a woman's feet was never going to be a good look.

The tune switched to a country and western ballad he remembered playing as a kid. It had been an old distraction. He'd taught himself to play harmonica while he waited alone for his mother to come back from one of her endless meetings.

A foster home would have offered more. Lissa's mention of her tonight had brought the memories back and reminded him why he didn't allow emotion to clutter his life.

His father had been no better at the parenting game. Predictably he'd tired of the marriage and lived a separate life under this very roof. But by some miracle they'd conceived Blake. What a joke.

He'd learned early on not to depend on others for emotional or any other kind of support. Janine had reinforced that learning in his late teens. *Love equals vulnerability.*

Women looking for more than the casual date soon discovered he wasn't that kind of guy. As long as they were on the same wavelength he was happy to indulge whatever games they wanted to play, but the moment he got a glimpse of those stars in their eyes he was off.

And now there was Lissa.

Too young, too inexperienced, too-delicate Lissa. He hadn't missed the flicker of real fear in her eyes when he'd backed her up against the wall just now and guilt sat uncomfortably alongside the roiling in his gut.

Definitely off-limits to guys like him.

The strip of golden sand was strewn with shells, driftwood and dead palm leaves where the rainforest met the sea. The heavy pounding at the back of his skull was gunfire and the sound of his boots on the hard-packed sand.

Blake looked over his shoulder.

Torque crouched on the sand, frozen.

Blake dodging bullets. Dragging him across the beach. Torque's cry as he fell, knocking him off balance. Rocks coming up to meet him as he fell...

'Blake. Blake, wake up.'

He jerked awake like a panic-stricken diver out of oxygen. Lissa's voice, her tone calm but firm and instantly grounding.

A wave of relief flooded over him as his eyes blinked open. Ghostly light from the muted TV screen lit the living room.

He was on the couch and she was perched on the arm rest, watching him with concern in those pretty eyes. He remembered coming out here, unable to find sleep in the study.

Relief quickly turned to a storm of humiliation and he started to lift his head, which felt like a ripe watermelon. *How long had she been watching him?*

'You okay?'

Her cool light fingers on his brow both soothed and embarrassed. A bloody rerun of last night.

He pushed her arm away. 'Yeah.' His mouth was dust dry. He didn't know if it was the result of being caught napping or the sight of her in nothing but that wispy white nightdress. In the TV's soft glow he could see the outline of her nipples against the sheer fabric.

He closed his eyes and imagined diving back into the cool, dark ocean.

'Are you still in pain?'

His eyes blinked open again. She was looking at his pack of prescription painkillers on the coffee table.

'No.' *Not the kind of pain you're referring to.* 'I'm fine.'

'You didn't sound fine.'

He swore silently to himself. Had he called out? Made an idiot of himself? Ignoring the vague residual dizziness, he pushed up, set his feet on the floor and said, 'How was the party? I didn't hear you come in.' He hadn't realised how he felt about her enjoying herself until he heard the sarcastic edge to his voice.

'If you didn't go, you'll never know.' She passed him a tumbler of water. 'Seems like you need this more than I do.'

He gulped half of it down, returned the glass to her. 'Thanks.'

Obviously in no hurry to go upstairs, she curled her feet beneath her and sipped at the water. 'Something horrible happened to bring you back to Oz after all this time. I've been wondering what.'

Right now he wondered the same thing about his choice of location to recuperate. He could have gone to Acapulco or Hawaii. Found some warm and willing local girl to recuperate with. But for some reason he'd yet to fathom, because it certainly wasn't for the love of family, he'd decided to return to Australia.

Bad things happened but he didn't want to talk about it. Not with the party girl who saw the world through a rainbow prism. What the hell would she know about real life? How could she ever understand what he did or why he did it? Nor did he want her to know. God knew, he wanted to protect her from all that.

And yet…he'd never had someone like Lissa interested enough in his life to ask. Maybe because he'd never been around a woman long enough. A strange warm sensation settled somewhere in the region of his heart.

'I'm not going to pretend I didn't hear you in your sleep. Post-traumatic stress isn't something to be ashamed of. Perhaps I could help,' she finished softly.

'*Post-traumatic stress?*' A rough laugh rasped up his throat. 'You don't know what the *hell* you're talking about. I get the occasional migraine, so what?' He pushed off the couch and headed for the stairs.

'Maybe you should let others do some looking out for you for a change,' she said behind him.

He reached the first step, didn't stop. 'With you around why would I need to?'

CHAPTER EIGHT

LISSA barely paused to breathe in the front garden's tropical scents as she stepped outside. The warm Mooloolaba morning wrapped around her but she barely noticed. A gazillion thoughts were running through her mind—*not* Blake and that kiss that had turned her inside out last night.

Although she did spare more than a passing thought for his nightmares. His haunted groans in the dark of night had chilled her to the bone. But unless and until he was willing to talk, what could she do? She shook her head. And he'd called her stubborn?

So for now Blake's living room was top priority. The living room was her *focus*. She had furniture and soft furnishings to select and order, paint to choose...

But she glanced down at the unfamiliar sharp staccato on the paved garden path and slowed to admire her sassy red sling-backs. Nice. They brought a smile to her lips. She'd not bought a thing for over three months. Even if they were only bargain basement, they were shiny and brand spanking new.

'Lissa.'

She heard her name spoken in that deep sexy drawl and saw Blake coming through the front gate. No sign of last night's terrors in those azure eyes. As he jogged across the lawn towards her every other thought flew out of her mind.

She came to a halt, her pulse doing a blip at the blinding sight of all that exposed bronzed skin. His upper arms gleamed with sweat, his navy blue vest-top was dark and damp. Short shorts revealed tanned, toned muscular thighs peppered with dark masculine hair.

Last night he'd pressed those thighs against hers.

She forgot she was on a mission. Forgot she had no time to waste, no time to linger over mere distractions. Even if the distraction was Blake Everett, with his musky scent wafting towards her. He looked like some sort of divine being sent from above. She blew out a heartfelt breath. Her shoes weren't the only things worth a second look around here.

'Wait up, I'm coming with you.' He was watching her as he approached and she knew by the way his eyes suddenly darkened that he was thinking about last night too. *You're not ready for what I'd like to do to you.*

Until he'd walked off.

Dragging her gaze away, she lifted her chin. His loss. 'No time,' she told him. She didn't want him with her, reminding her of whatever shared delights he'd decided she wasn't ready for and taking her mind off what she needed to buy. She keyed the remote to raise the roller door, then unlocked her car and tossed her bag on the front passenger seat.

'Are you sure that's all?' He studied her far too astutely while he lifted a bottle of water to his lips.

'What else would it—?'

'Blake?'

Lissa turned at the interruption to see Gilda from next door slipping through the front gate.

'Blake?' she called again. 'It *is* you!'

'Gilda Matilda!' His face broke into a broad relaxed smile, something he hadn't bestowed on Lissa, she noted with a curious feeling in the pit of her stomach as he changed direction and jogged towards the woman.

Flawlessly made-up, their neighbour wore a stunning white

sundress that no doubt came from some exclusive European collection. Lissa, in her new off-the-rack red skirt and cream jacket, instantly felt outclassed.

Blake leaned down, dropped a kiss on her cheek. 'You're still living here, I see.'

'Yes. And about time you came home, you long-lost sailor, you.' The dark-haired woman returned the kiss and gave him a heartfelt hug, the clutch of rings on the third finger of her left hand sparkling in the light. She turned and smiled Lissa's way. 'Hello, Lissa. How are you? I didn't realise you two knew each other.'

'Hi, Gilda. Yes, we knew each other in Surfers. It was a long time ago.' She glanced at Blake and saw something flicker in his gaze before he turned his attention back to their neighbour.

Lissa wandered towards them. She wanted to watch their interaction and see if it was just herself he didn't let in on his life's details.

Gilda beamed up at him. 'Well, what extraordinary activities have you been up to all this time?'

'I can see what *you've* been up to.'

Neatly diverting attention away from himself. Again.

His gaze dropped to the woman's gently rounded belly. 'Congratulations. Or have you popped out a couple of others since I last saw you?'

She laughed, breathless and happy. 'No. This is our first.' Her gaze softened and turned inwards and her voice grew almost reverent. 'It's a miracle. Fifteen years of trying and now I'm six months along. I still can't believe it.'

'You've waited a long time, Gil. Enjoy it.'

'Oh, I am. Every minute.' Her smile flashed wider. 'I'm in the throes of preparing the nursery. It's a girl and I can't decide whether to go with traditional pink or something completely unexpected. Whatever we decide, it's got to be something spectacular. But I guess you men are all the same.' She flapped a hand and smiled knowingly at Lissa. 'Put off by women's talk of nurseries.'

'Maybe your neighbour can help you out.'

'Oh?'

'Lissa's an interior designer and, believe me, you'll want to see her ideas.' He cast a conspiratorial smile Lissa's way. 'She's working on my living room at present, but I'm sure she'll find time to fit you into her schedule.'

'Really?' Gilda's eyes lit up. 'I had no idea, Lissa. What a timely surprise. And I'd love your input.'

Lissa's spirits soared and she cast Blake a grateful glance. What better opportunity would come her way than the chance to impress this wealthy suburban socialite with her expertise?

'I'd be happy to give you some options to consider, Gilda. Would this afternoon be a convenient time for me to look at the room?'

'Oh, that'd be wonderful. Shall we say 2:00 p.m.?'

'That'll be fine. I'll see you then.'

Gilda paused, her eyes darting between both of them as if deciding whether they were an item or not. 'Are you two doing anything tomorrow evening? I'm having a little party and I'd love it if you could both come.'

'We'd be delighted,' Blake answered for both of them.

'Can we bring something?' Lissa offered and immediately wished she'd kept her naïve mouth shut. Gilda didn't do anything so simple as pot-luck dinners.

'Just your wallets,' she said with a grin. 'It's a fundraiser for childhood cancer awareness, so it's gold tie or gold ribbon for you, Blake, and a gold dress, Lissa.'

Oh. Not even a semi-formal occasion then, but one of her famous extravaganzas. Obviously Gilda assumed everyone had a gold gown hanging in the closet. Her society friends probably did. Lissa wanted to go. It was an exciting, timely opportunity, but who'd give her a second glance in her chain store's little black dress?

But Blake…he wasn't a party kind of guy. She could see it in his stance, in the set of his jaw. He'd accepted because he knew it was a chance for her to make some contacts.

'About tomorrow night…' she began as they waved Gilda goodbye and walked towards the car. 'I—'

'I suspect this type of party's not exactly your thing but—'

'That's *not* what I was going to say.' At the car door, she swung round to look at him. 'If you'd rather not attend, I can go alone.'

He stared her down. 'Not a chance.' His fingers curved over the door frame as he held it open for her. 'Now hop in. You've got shopping to do.'

She wanted to thank him but she knew now that it would make him uncomfortable.

'Why couldn't it be a simple black tie dinner?' she moaned, climbing in. 'I don't have a suitable dress and I'm so busy today.' She slid the key into the ignition. 'I have an appointment to look at office furniture…' she glanced at her watch '…in half an hour.'

'Not much point looking at outfitting the shop if you don't have clients. You've got two days. Plenty of time to look at dresses.'

'What about your room? That's a priority.'

'You can do both. I've every confidence in you.'

'Gold, for heaven's sake.' She turned the key and the old engine, badly in need of a service, coughed into life. 'Where will I find a gold dress?' More to the point, where would she find one that didn't cost an arm and a leg?

'You're a woman, you'll find one. Use the new account. We'll claim it as a business expense.'

'We can do that?'

He shook his head. 'Let me handle the finances for now,

Lissa. And see if you can find me a gold tie while you're at it,' he said. And swung the door shut.

Lissa pulled into the drive at two minutes to two. Leaving her supplies in the car, she rushed inside. Blake was nowhere to be seen so she grabbed her portfolio, then hurried next door to Gilda's impressive home.

'Hello again, Lissa, it's good of you to come.' Gilda held the door wide. 'I'm so looking forward to hearing your ideas.'

Lissa smiled all the way down to her toes. 'I'm happy to help out.'

Gilda ushered Lissa through to the spacious living area overlooking the pool. Every surface from the polished furniture to the marble floors and gold fittings gleamed. Urns of flowers filled the air with fresh fragrance. A cleaning service was in full swing on the patio.

'Preparations for tomorrow night,' Gilda explained, indicating a seat on a silk upholstered couch.

'I'm surprised you have the time, being pregnant and all.' Then again, having a cleaning service no doubt helped.

She set her portfolio carefully on the marble topped coffee table and said, 'Before we get started, I'd like to do my bit and donate a portion of my services for the nursery makeover towards your cause tomorrow night.'

A pot of steaming aromatic coffee and a jug of orange juice sat on a tray on the sideboard along with a plate of Kourabiedes, Greek shortbread biscuits that Lissa loved. Gilda picked it up and set it down in front of them. 'That's a thoughtful gesture, Lissa, are you sure?'

'Of course.' She knew without asking that Blake would be the kind of man who'd wholeheartedly approve.

'Thank you so much, you're very generous.' Gilda lifted the pot. 'Coffee?'

'Yes, please.'

'It's lovely to see Blake back home again after all this time.' Her voice softened at the mention of his name.

'You two seem close.' Lissa took the proffered cup, hoping to hide the colour she could feel in her cheeks. She shouldn't have asked. It was none of her business. She was here in a professional capacity.

'Yes. We are.' Gilda watched Lissa with a woman's understanding in her eyes while she poured herself a glass of juice. 'You probably don't know, because he's not the kind of man to tell, but he saved my life.'

'Really?' Lissa's cup stopped halfway to her lips. 'What happened?'

'Blake was living on the houseboat at the time. I slipped on the pool surround, broke my leg and fell in. It was the housekeeper's day off. If he hadn't heard my calls and come to my rescue I'd have drowned.'

'Oh, my goodness. You were lucky.'

'Indeed I was. It could have stopped there, but no. He helped me through the two months when I was housebound on crutches. The housekeeper came in daily, of course, and I had a nurse for a while, but Blake provided the company.

'We were both keen chess players and loved adventure movies so that passed time, but, more than that, we were both lonely. Stefan was away on business for weeks at a time and Blake's father…' She waved him off. 'And his mother was too busy to notice.'

Gilda's mouth pursed as if she'd bitten into a sour pomegranate. 'As much as I respected Rochelle's charitable work, I couldn't come to grips with how she neglected her only child.' She shook her head, setting her earrings jangling. 'There was Rochelle with a son she'd never taken the time to get to know, and I'd have given anything for a baby yet I couldn't get pregnant.'

Blake had been a neglected child? No wonder he'd closed

up when she'd praised his mother's tireless charity work. Yet he'd never said a bad word about her.

And here was Lissa with a brother who'd given up his teenage years for her to make a loving home, to keep her safe. Blake hadn't had that security, nor obviously had he known the feeling of being loved as he grew up.

'So there we were,' Gilda continued. 'A bit of an odd pair to the rest of the world. But there was honesty and I like to think there was a trust between us despite the difference in our ages. Stefan thinks the world of him.'

Lissa felt an odd twinge around her heart. It seemed he wasn't an island. He confided in someone after all. Just not Lissa. And why would he? she asked herself. The last time she'd seen him she'd been thirteen.

And when it came right down to it, what would be the point? He was leaving.

'Then he joined the navy.'

Gilda's words had Lissa's thoughts spinning in another direction. 'Was that a sudden decision?'

'He spoke of it often enough, but in the end, yes, it was.'

Janine.

Gilda eyed Lissa over her glass and both knew what wasn't being said. 'You can be sure if he'd made a mistake he'd have stayed to fix it.'

Lissa looked down at her cup. Maybe he had stayed. A couple of days, a quick private trip to a clinic, problem solved. But even as the thought came to her, she knew it couldn't be true. She'd learned more about Blake in the past couple of days than she'd ever known. It wasn't in his nature to run away from his problems.

She could feel the other woman's gaze and set her eggshell-fragile gold-rimmed cup on its saucer with the faintest tremor. 'Of course he would have.'

She wasn't here for a history lesson and she wasn't going

to talk to Gilda about her own relationship with Blake. That would be unprofessional.

She reached for her portfolio. 'Why don't you have a look through this? Then you can show me the nursery and we can start things happening.'

When Blake arrived home early evening, he found Lissa cross-legged on the floor in the living room surrounded by a maze of sketches, designs and scribbled notes.

She looked up as he approached, taking in his sand-covered legs. 'Hi. You've been to the beach, I see.'

'Thought I'd test the surf—wind's up today and there was a good swell.' He sat down opposite her, against the wall, plonked his damp towel and two boxes on the floor. Now he'd made up his mind Lissa was off-limits, he concentrated on thinking of her as a friend. A business partner. Easier said than done when her perfume filled his nostrils and his eyes couldn't seem to focus on anything but her tanned knees. 'How did it go with Gilda?'

'Very well.' Her eyes glowed with enthusiasm. 'She's going with a fairy-tale theme. Pastel colours. I saw this gorgeous little pumpkin-shaped cot today…I can't wait to get started.'

'If you want to postpone this room—'

'I can do both. You told me so and it's good practice. I've already organised the painters here for next week and the furniture's been ordered.'

For the first time since he'd come back he took a good look at the room, visions of the way it used to look swimming before his eyes. 'I can't wait to see this transformed. It always reminds me of…'

She looked up. 'What?' she asked softly.

'Dad used to have his poker nights in here. Four nights a week. I remember the first night I came to live with him. I was fourteen. Mum had gone overseas so I was sent to Dad's.' He leaned his head back against the wall, the bad old memories coming thick and fast. 'Dad had forgotten to pick me up at the bus so I walked. With my luggage.' He closed his eyes, felt the old tension grab at the base of his skull.

'Go on,' she urged. Her voice was gentle. Oddly calming, like the trickle of water over a moss-covered rock. So easy to let it flow over him.

'The place was a garbage tip. Beer bottles, pizza boxes, spilled cigarette ash, you name it. I thought after his buddies left he'd clean it up, but no. It was still there a week later.

'The rest of the house was just as bad. In the end I couldn't stand it so I asked if I could live on the houseboat. He was more than happy with the arrangement. I taught myself to cook. At least I could study in peace...'

A long silence followed. 'I never knew my father,' Lissa said into the hiatus.

He opened his eyes. 'What?'

'That man you knew wasn't my father. My biological father was just passing through town one summer. I must have looked liked him because Dad hated me. I was a reminder of my mother's infidelity.'

She smiled suddenly. 'This sounds like True Confession time.'

He smiled back, feeling as if a load had been lifted off his shoulders. Feeling something like companionship. He'd never told anyone his troubles. Somehow Lissa had got him to talk. To open up. And it felt good. Freeing. Connected. 'How about we go eat some pizza? I saw a live band setting up in an outdoor café on the esplanade. Oh, wait up.' He picked up the boxes, reached over and set them in front of her. 'This first.'

Lissa reached for the larger one. 'What is it?' When he didn't answer, she opened the flaps. Her jewellery box sat on the top. 'Oh...' Eyes filling, she pulled it out and opened it. It was still damp but she lifted out the bluebird brooch. 'This was Mum's. You rescued my things.' She could barely see him through the tears.

'I had the boat moved yesterday while you were at the shop. I didn't get everything, most of it was too far gone, but the stuff in the box was salvageable. And what I thought you might like.'

She ran her hands over a white porcelain bowl with blue dolphins around the edge. It had been a gift from Crystal when she'd moved here. He'd thought enough to sort through her things. 'Thank you. So much.'

She opened the other box. It was full of new lingerie. All different colours. Sexy as sin. She sifted through the silky bras and panties, her cheeks blooming with heat. She found two nightgowns. A teal blue and a deep gold.

'I noticed you didn't buy enough stuff yesterday,' he said, his voice oddly gruff.

The heat intensified. 'How did you know my size?'

'I checked the ones you bought. If you'll forgive me for looking.'

'Oh, yes…and they're beautiful.' She bit her lip. 'I don't know what to say.'

'Your smile's enough.' He reached out a hand, lifted her chin up. 'You should smile more often—with those eyes, like you're doing now.' For a fleeting moment his gaze turned almost reverent.

And she felt her heart melt.

Then he pushed up, as if uncomfortable with the moment. 'Let's go eat.'

CHAPTER NINE

For this evening, at least, it was enough to simply share pizza and enjoy each other's company while the waves thumped on the beach. To see the ocean change from aqua to indigo to black and to watch Blake finally relax as they listened to the jazz quartet.

It gave Lissa time to think about what Blake had told her about his father. No wonder he was obsessed with order and tidiness. She resolved to make more of an effort while she was staying in his house.

When the band packed up, they drove home and went their separate ways to bed. The ever-present hum between them was still there, but also a feeling that barriers had been lowered a little. As if a bridge had been crossed.

Lissa spent the following day working on the living room and plans for Gilda's nursery. Blake offered to be at the shop in the morning to receive the office supplies she'd ordered. He refused her suggestion to accompany her shopping in the afternoon and went surfing instead.

The last item on her list was what to wear to Gilda's party.

He should have insisted on going shopping with her, Blake decided that evening as he stood at the bottom of the staircase looking up.

He resisted the urge to loosen the gold bow tie that threatened to strangle him as he stared at the woman descending the stairs.

No way he'd have agreed to the skinny tube of shimmering gold lamé and its row upon row of bright coins that jingled and winked in the light as she moved. What there was of it. Her 'find' was strapless and covered precious little of those sun-kissed thighs that he'd thought about constantly since that first night on the houseboat.

His brow wrinkled. Except now she was coming closer he could see that those thighs seemed to be dusted with something like…gold dust… She'd threaded gold ribbons through her hair and piled it on top of her head and he noticed her shoulders gleamed with the same fine gold glitter as her thighs. Strappy gold stilettos completed the look.

An uncomfortable heat burst into flame below the surface of his skin and spread all over his body like a rash. How was he going to get through the evening without thinking about what other priceless treasures she had hidden beneath that slinky scrap of fabric that looked as if she'd simply wound it around her? He was going to spend the whole night wondering if it came off as easily.

'What do you think?' she said, reaching the bottom of the stairs.

'It's…certainly eye-catching.' Not to mention snagging on a few other sensitive body parts.

'That's the idea.' She shimmied like a belly-dancer and the whole thing glittered and jingled. 'Not bad for a few moments' work and a couple of quick threads, huh?'

Quick threads? He swallowed. It was held together with a few threads? 'You…constructed it yourself?'

'I'm not wasting money when I don't have to. I found it in an off-cut bin at a belly-dance studio.' She held up a hand and thin gold bangles danced along her arm. 'No, don't ask how it holds together. And no, it's not going to unravel. At least I hope not.'

By God, so did he.

'But just in case...' She flicked at a string of tiny gold safety pins tucked discreetly into the top.

Music, voices and a tinkle of feminine laughter drifted from next door as she reached down to adjust a strap on her sandal then straightened. 'Still, I hardly think I'll be noticed among the Beautiful People.'

Blake gave his head a mental shake. It was she who was beautiful, and, going on his memory of these charity dos, the majority of party-goers were generally over fifty. She was going to give some old geezer a heart attack.

If he wasn't careful she was going to give *him* a heart attack.

'Nice look.' Her gaze slid over his dark suit rather too slowly for his comfort. 'Do you get a lot of wear out of that attire in the navy? Lots of military functions to attend, admirals to salute? Wives and daughters to charm?'

He didn't miss the glimmer of dark in those clear eyes at her pointed mention of the last.

'But of course,' she ran on before he could get a word in. She shook her head and a single auburn curl beside her ear bobbled. 'You'd wear one of those gorgeous naval dress uniforms, wouldn't you? All blinding white with gold buttons.' Her gaze clouded momentarily as if she saw him dressed so.

And if they didn't get going, he was going to have to reach out and smooth that curl behind her ear...and then...his stomach tightened...they'd be in a world of trouble. He turned away, towards the door. 'Shall we go?'

Lissa tried not to look impressed but Gilda and Stefan's magnificent mansion had been transformed into a Grecian paradise. In the balmy air, multicoloured lanterns hung overhead and reflected like fireworks in the sapphire pool while guests wearing the latest in gold designer fashion feasted on a multitude of delicacies and drank champagne from sparkling crystal glasses.

The patio doors had been flung open and, inside, tall orchid spikes speared from gilt-edged vases set on ornate polished mahogany or marble pedestals, their exotic scents mingling with expensive French perfume. Somewhere a blues singer accompanied a clarinet, crooning come-hither World War Two songs.

She didn't have time to absorb it all because as soon as they arrived they were handed drinks and Lissa was whisked away by her hostess to meet a trio of women who'd known Blake's mother, wealthy middle-aged matrons dripping with diamonds. And gold. It was like being in the house of Midas.

Blake was still watching her as she cast him a backward glance. He raised his glass. *Enjoy the evening*, he seemed to say. *I intend to.* From the corner of her eye she saw why: tall, blonde and busty heading his way.

So there was Lissa, hearing all about Muriel someone's latest fashion disaster while waiting for a lull in the conversation so she could get a word in about her business—*their* business—while he indulged in…whatever it was he was doing behind her back.

'Oh, and did you hear that the Bakers from Surfers heard Rochelle's son was coming and cancelled at the last minute?'

Lissa's ears pricked up.

But at sharp glances from her friends, the woman who'd delivered the news found a sudden interest in the bottom of her crystal flute. 'Oops. Sorry.'

The words, obviously aimed Lissa's way and tossed out with malicious amusement, stunned her. Then filled her with anger. A red-hot ball in her chest. She felt it build and build until she felt as if she might explode.

This was Blake they were maligning. Who'd risked his life for fourteen years and suffered God only knew what horrors to keep their country safe. A man she'd learned was much more than she'd ever given him credit for. Once upon a time she'd listened to the rumours too. She didn't know the circumstances with Janine. She didn't need to—she knew Blake.

And she'd trust him with her life.

The sudden realisation stunned her anew. She'd never thought it possible to feel that way about a man again. Armed with that knowledge, she took a sip from her glass before seizing the opportunity in the lull to ask, 'Are you talking about Janine?'

There was a startled 'Was she a friend of yours?'

'No.' She looked straight into the other woman's eyes. 'But Blake is.'

More glance-swapping. Frowns exchanged. A conspiracy of silence. Awkward moment.

'I hate innuendoes and gossip, don't you?' She tilted her champagne flute towards the women, looking at each one in turn. 'Especially when we all know it's based on lies and hearsay and spread by ignorance.'

For a few tense seconds there wasn't a murmur. Not so much as a flicker of movement from any of them. It was as if they'd been turned to stone. Or solid gold.

Then the oldest of the three smiled slowly. 'Well said, my dear. I like a girl who's not afraid to stand up for herself.' Looking Lissa up and down, she nodded approvingly. 'My name's Jocelyn. Rochelle Everett was one of my closest friends. So tell us how you met Blake and then we'd love to hear all about your new business.' She turned to the others. 'Wouldn't we, ladies?'

Lissa mingled with the crowd, feeling extraordinarily satisfied. Jocelyn had given her a business card and told her to make an appointment to look at renovating her kitchen. She made two other appointments with potential clients over the next hour.

Finally, excusing herself from the airless room, she made her way outside to the patio and the younger set. A couple of women in gold bikinis were splashing about in the pool and laughing.

And like any other unattached male, where else would Blake be but watching on from the decking? Tossing their big plastic ball back to them with a grin?

The pain that twisted beneath her ribcage was nothing to do with the way they were deliberately throwing it in his direction, nor the fact that he was obviously enjoying the attention. It was just the way she'd tied the length of fabric too tight beneath her breasts.

He must have felt her glare because he looked up and their eyes met over the cavorting mermaids. He'd removed his jacket and his white shirt clung to his body like a second skin, making his skin appear even more bronzed. She refused to notice. *Fun for some.* She was sweating contacts and appointments while he was sweating…bimbos.

Turning away, she headed for the nearest waiter.

What? Blake mouthed, watching her. Too late. She was already stalking off, disappearing among the crowd, her undulating gold-wrapped hips a magnificent memory.

He rolled shoulders suddenly gone tense. He'd kept out of the way to give Lissa a chance to do her thing. He knew it was important to her that she make a success of this on her own. She wanted independence. He was giving it to her. Though he had to admit he had no inclination to schmooze with his mother's cronies unless they found him. To his vexation, a few of them had. But he'd played nice. For Lissa's sake.

And all he'd got was a glare for his trouble.

Frowning, he skirted the pool in pursuit. What had he done to tick her off?

He caught sight of her near one of the glittering supper

tables, her expression animated as she spoke to an elderly woman with lavender hair, and found himself stalling. To watch her, simply watch her.

The grown-up Lissa wasn't what he'd expected. And different from the other women he'd associated with over the years. She didn't fawn all over him; she had too much dignity. Nor did she give herself unrealistic airs. She was down-to-earth. She had guts. Moxy. Pride. When she'd lost her boat and almost everything she'd owned, she'd picked herself up and moved on.

And...*for pity's sake*...when it came down to sheer sexuality, she attracted him like no other.

At that moment some of the guests nearby moved away, giving him a clear view of those attributes. Feminine curves. Shapely legs.

How would those thighs feel wrapped around his waist?

Lust clutched him low and hard and his vision blurred. He grabbed a beer from a waiter's tray as he headed towards her. When he looked her way again a dude in a shiny gold suit had struck up a conversation with her.

Blake scowled. Typical indoors type—pale skin and smooth manicured hands. Wrong haircut. Apparently it didn't bother Lissa because her eyes sparkled and that luscious mouth curved as she laughed at something he said.

Then, as if she felt the heat of Blake's gaze, she turned her head slightly and their eyes met. A ribbon of heat arced across the space between them.

But then Midas Man shifted, leaned closer, blocking Blake's view. Simmering with impatience, he threw back his beer, plunked the near-empty glass on a marble pedestal bedecked with gold-painted leaves and closed in.

He circled behind her so that he could lay his hand on the middle of her back and lean in close to catch the heat of her skin and inhale her scent. *To claim possession*. He felt her tense beneath his touch. Then she jerked round, and those stunning eyes blinked. Just once.

'Blake.'

She sounded surprised. As if she wasn't expecting to see him there. Damn it. Clearly that look they'd exchanged less than thirty seconds ago hadn't meant what he'd thought it meant. His impatience reached flash point.

Ignoring her conversation partner, Blake leaned even closer, so that his lips grazed the tip of her ear, and murmured, 'We need to leave.'

'Now? But—'

'Something's come up.'

'Oh? What?'

A heart-pounding beat. The tiny space between them crackled with something like static electricity. He knew she knew by the spark of realisation in her eyes, which were focused carefully on his. 'Oh.'

'And it needs immediate attention.'

She turned to the Midas Man. 'Excuse me…'

Her voice trailed off as Blake grabbed her hand and towed her away.

'What are you doing?' she muttered breathlessly.

'Saving you from terminal boredom.'

She shot a quick look behind her. 'That's mean, he was very sweet…not to mention mega-rich with a mansion to renovate. And we're here in a professional capacity…'

'Don't change the subject,' he snapped. His pulse was drumming in his ears. 'We're here as Gilda's friends.'

'What subject?'

Ignoring her question, he continued tugging her away from the crowd towards a wide chandeliered hallway, past alcoves where Grecian alabaster goddesses posed until he came to a narrower passage. He found the nearest closed door, pulled her inside and slammed it shut behind them. The party noise evaporated. A lone gold candle flickered on the bathroom vanity and he got a glimpse of his own reflection and Lissa's wide eyes before he turned away.

The sound of the lock turning sounded preternaturally loud in the sudden silence and he heard her sharp indrawn breath as she pressed a hand to her chest.

'What's wrong?'

'I... You startled me for a moment.'

'You startle easily, party girl,' he murmured. He could feel the warmth of her body beneath her dress, the silken slide of her arm as he twisted her so that she was wedged between him and the door.

'What was all that stuff you said earlier about drumming up clients?' In the dim light he saw her eyes spark as she looked up at him and her voice took on a clipped edge. 'I noticed *you* weren't d—'

'Shut up and kiss me,' he said, and laid his lips on that luscious mouth as he'd wanted to do all evening.

CHAPTER TEN

As HIS lips claimed hers, everything else flew out of Lissa's mind except that this was Blake kissing her and she was kissing him back. His hands on her shoulders, her waist, her hips. His body heat searing her from neck to knee and every place between. His forest-fresh cologne and the musky scent of clean male sweat.

But mostly it was the way he kissed her. Hot with impatience, rich with desire. And with a fast-burning energy that threatened to spontaneously combust her right where she stood. His tongue plunged between her lips then withdrew, and again, making love to her mouth over and over until she felt her legs turning to jelly.

Somehow her desperate arms found their way around his neck, and she clung to him as if he were the one dependable reality in a world gone momentarily crazy.

He lifted his head and watched her through heavy-lidded eyes as he slid one hard palm between her thighs. Anticipation danced along her nerve endings, heat shimmered on her skin and she shivered all over. 'Yes…'

He continued to watch her as his hand moved higher. As his long fingers found the edge of her panties and crept beneath. As his thumb stroked her swollen sex, just once. Liquid heat rushed to her core and she sucked in a sharp breath as her intimate flesh quivered. 'Oh, *yes*.' Her head fell back against the door and her eyes slid shut.

'Do you like that?' His breath tickled as he nibbled her ear lobe.

'You know...a woman...who doesn't?' She wondered vaguely whether she was going to hyperventilate.

He stroked her again, then dipped a finger inside her. Drew it out slowly—a long smooth glide that sent her soaring half-way to the moon. He slid in once more. Two fingers. Deeper, more insistent.

Ribbons of colour played behind her eyelids, she felt the familiar rippling sensation building, building... So soon...a mere touch and she was already on the edge...

'Look at me,' he demanded, his voice harsh.

As the wave crashed over her and her internal muscles contracted around his fingers she opened her eyes and tumbled into his gaze. Candle-light flickered over his features and the room smelled of lilacs. 'Yes, yes, yes-s-s.' She felt herself start to slide down the wall and clung tighter to his neck.

'Gotcha.' With his hands beneath her bottom, he lifted her so that she was pinned against the door. She started wrapping her legs around his waist until the harsh sound of fabric ripping filled the room.

'Oops.' Her slightly hysterical, trembly laugh seemed to ricochet off the tiled walls.

They both heard the tap on the door and turned to stone, Blake's hands clamped on her bottom.

'Excuse me...' An elderly woman's voice.

'Uh-oh,' Lissa whispered. 'Now we're in trouble.'

Another knock, louder. 'Is everything all right in there?'

'Everything's fine,' Blake answered smoothly.

Before Lissa could disengage her arms from around his neck, he was fumbling for the pins at her bodice. His hands brushed her breast as he worked. Her nipples took no account of the fact that she and Blake were locked in a bathroom and some old lady was right outside the door probably waiting to use the loo, and puckered up even more tightly against his palm.

He pressed the pins into her hand, then stepped back to give her room to fasten the frayed edges, but her fingers shook so badly she barely managed the task. 'I'm not sure it'll hold for long.'

'It doesn't need to.' His voice was tight and gruff as he took her firmly by the arm, unlocked the door. 'You first.'

'Why me?' she whispered back. Oh. She unlocked the door, pulled it open.

Gilda was waiting with a concerned elderly lady hovering behind her. 'Oh, Lissa. Blake…?' Her voice rose slightly on the last. 'Margaret heard noises…'

Lissa stifled a nervous giggle that bubbled up.

Blake stepped behind her, his hands on her shoulders, and she felt an immediate surge of guilty embarrassment. She knew her face proclaimed to the world what she'd just been enjoying. Heat climbed into her cheeks. She didn't dare look down at the hem of her dress.

But Blake, cool and in control, at least to outward appearances, said, 'Wardrobe malfunction,' his voice betraying none of the huskiness and dark passion she'd heard moments ago. 'I'm taking Lissa home.'

'Oh…that's probably best.' A tiny line creased Gilda's brow. Obviously the shredded reason for their sudden departure wasn't apparent to her, even if their exit from the bathroom together left little doubt as to what they'd been doing.

'Thank you for coming, and thank you, Blake, for your very generous cheque.'

'You're welcome. I hope it'll do some good.' He dropped his hands and edged Lissa along with a firm palm at her back, obviously mindful of the fragility of those pins and her super-stiletto shoes. 'Thanks for inviting us.'

'Um,' Lissa agreed, vaguely. Her power of speech seemed to have deserted her. "Night.'

The moment they were away from prying eyes he swung her into his arms and carried her down the paved path. Under the street light his jaw was rigid, his eyes focused dead ahead. She could hear his heart thumping against her ear as he strode to the front door, keyed the security code and shouldered the door open.

He flicked on a light and they made it as far as the second stair—not far at all—before he bent his head and touched his brow to hers and said, 'Lissa,' in a strangled voice that spoke of barely restrained control.

He released her in such a way that her body slid slowly down the front of his, her feet landing on the step above where he stood. His lips were pressed together tight, eyes blazing with a passion that seared all the way through to her crazily beating heart and she wondered that it didn't stop altogether.

But then he said, 'Go on up to bed.'

Her heart did stop then, with a terrifying jolt before resuming its crazy rhythm. He didn't mean that. He *couldn't* mean that. Not after that mind-blowing trip to the moon he'd given her. Not with those eyes, not with that steel rod she'd felt as she'd slid down his rigid torso.

You're not ready for what I'd like to do to you.

Maybe she *should* go while she had the chance. Flee straight up those stairs to her room and lock the door tight.

Her legs barely held her upright but she remained where she was. This was Blake, and a night of pleasure in his arms beckoned. She stared him down. 'I'm not tired.'

A muscle in his jaw tightened and he growled through clenched teeth. 'Go, Lissa. Before I do something we'll both regret in the morning.'

'I'm not going anywhere.' Regrets were not on her agenda.

'You want me,' she said, and watched his eyes turn to smoke. 'And I want you.'

If they made love, she was going to fall hard. She was risking her heart. But hadn't her heart been his all along? 'I've always wanted you.'

She felt him go still beneath her palm. His entire body seemed to turn to stone. *That's right, Blake, think about that not-so-little confession.*

The impact of her words took a moment to sink in. 'Sweet heaven,' he groaned softly, and closed his eyes. 'You were only thirteen last time I saw you. For God's sake, go. Go now.'

'Blake, what I'm trying to say here is, it's not a whim,' she continued. 'It's n—'

'Do you realise what would have happened back in that room if Nanna Margaret hadn't knocked on the door and given me a moment to regain some sense? I'd have taken you where you stood without a moment's hesitation and to hell with the rest of the world.'

Lava geysered through her veins and she thought for one moment she might faint with the thrill.

'And with not one damn thought of protection,' he finished, his voice scraping like rough stone over her senses.

Her mind spun back to those rumours. The rumours she refused to believe. The rumours she'd condemned only hours ago. But even so, the heat cooled and congealed in her blood because there was one indisputable fact—he *had* been dating Janine.

Had he lost control with her? Had he been so driven, so lost, so crazy hot for her that he'd forgotten birth control? Sharp images of his hands, his mouth on the girl's flesh, that hard masculine *unprotected* part of him plunging into her where she stood tore at Lissa.

'And now?' Her throat was clogged, her voice tight. 'What, you've suddenly developed a conscience in the last few minutes?'

'No.' His eyes blazed. 'That's the problem, Lissa. You make me crazy. When I'm with you, when I'm anywhere near you, I don't *have* a conscience. And I don't seem to be able to function rationally.'

'And you need to be in control at all times.'

His non-answer and the blue flame in his eyes told her all she needed to know, but she could lure him over to the dark side. She could. 'You've been trying *not* to wonder how this dress comes off all night, haven't you?'

Blake didn't move a muscle. His eyes...it was as if they were glued in place. He could *not* tear them away from those sun-spangled thighs. The twist of gold and the curves beneath.

'It's one long strip of fabric,' she said. 'Like a scarf. You start at the bottom—or the top—and unwrap it. Like a birth-day gift.'

Birthday gifts? His mother hadn't believed in such indulgences. Instead he'd been allowed to choose which charity he wanted to donate to. 'I'm warning you now, I don't do emotion, Lissa.'

'Fine. We won't do emotion. We'll just have sex.' She stepped out of her shoes.

Still facing him, she took a backward step, up one stair. Slowly, hypnotically, making the little coins on her dress jingle and drawing his gaze up and over her flat belly and full breasts. It also caused the air around her to eddy, bringing her sweet and sinfully tempting perfume to his nose.

The reincarnation of Circe, he thought, seducing him with a feast of the senses. Weaving a spell around him with those captivating eyes. Drawing him closer. Making his hand reach out in front of him as if it belonged to someone else.

But it wasn't someone else's fingers that tingled as they touched that warm flesh once more. And it was his hand that burned as it traced an invisible line inside the fabric and up the smooth line of her leg. Ankle, calf, the back of her knee. The long firm length of her outer thigh.

His fingers retraced their journey down to the tattered hem of her dress and closed over the fabric, knuckles brushing her skin and feeling the quiver run through her like a tiny electric current.

Need. This ferocious and urgent and *soul-deep* need... He'd never experienced anything remotely like it. One yank and he could have her naked. Sprawled on the stairs while he plunged into her, her precious innocence gone in a few seconds flat.

She deserved better. So much better. He closed his eyes briefly, then looked at her. 'I don't want to hurt you.'

A flash of something lit her eyes and a small frown puckered her brow. 'What do you mean...hurt me?'

'You're a virgin...and this...this... It isn't—'

Her eyes widened. *'Virgin?'*

'You mean you're not?' He stared at her while his mind reeled and his whole body tightened.

'Whatever gave you that idea?'

'You said... Never mind.'

'Blake.' A smile stole across her lips. 'I'm not a virgin. I haven't been one in quite a while. I've had a few lovers in my time—just don't tell Jared that. You really need to stop thinking of me as that kid you knew.'

'I don't,' he muttered, his blood surging south, pulse hammering in his ears. 'Believe me, I don't.'

He wound the lower end of the fabric around his hand, tightened his fingers into a fist and tugged. 'Come here.'

But she shook her head. 'I feel like a swim.' Her smile was wicked as she stepped past him on the step, twirling a circle as she went, the gold strip unravelling like a streamer behind her.

She continued whirling across the room towards the patio, shedding any inhibitions he'd thought she had along with her scarf. He saw that she was wearing a tiny triangle of tarnished gold lace, her luscious breasts spilling out of a matching strapless bra.

She ran out of scarf and jerked to a stop. Blake growled low in his throat and walked towards her, gathering up the fabric. Reeling her in. But before he got within reach she tossed her end to the floor and was off, flinging the patio doors wide.

Her bare bottom flashed in the light spilling from the house as she danced across the slate tiles. At the edge of the pool she turned and met his gaze. Peeled the bra off and threw it over her shoulder. Slid her hands down her hips, taking her gold thong with them.

He felt a momentary disappointment that she'd robbed him of the opportunity to perform the task himself, then again, he shrugged. What a view. He breathed out a sigh. *Per*fection. Every tempting hollow, every inviting curve.

'Stay right where you...' she smiled at him, then stepped backwards into the water '...are,' he finished.

She bobbed up again almost immediately, her eyes laughing. 'Feels good.' Her voice was as sultry as the night. 'Don't you want to feel good, Blake?'

Oh, yeah. 'Get out so I can see you.'

'Sure you don't want to join me in the water?'

'Maybe later.' He beckoned her. 'Out. Now.'

She shrugged and moved to the ladder, climbed out. Water sluiced off her body, leaving droplets clinging to her skin like diamonds, her dripping hair a dark crimson threaded with gold ribbons.

He didn't take his eyes off the glorious sight as he quickly stripped down to skin. He saw her eyes widen at the sight of his throbbing erection, felt the hot stroke of her gaze clear across the patio.

His mouth watered at the sight of her glistening nipples puckered up with the pool's chill. As he watched water gathered at the rosy tips and dripped onto the slate. Urgency whipped through his body like a loosened high-tension wire in a blustery wind, but he refused to hurry.

She was the birthday cake he'd never had and he was going to take his own sweet time over her and indulge. Before they were done he was going to sample every delectable square centimetre.

He stepped onto the soft emerald grass. 'Come here.'

She moved towards him with that same stunning grace he'd seen when she'd danced. And then she was there, looking up at him with wide turquoise eyes.

'You're a temptress, you know that, don't you?'

'Uh-huh.' She was breathing fast, her breasts rising and falling. 'Did I tempt you?'

'Oh, yeah.' He smoothed his hands over her damp shoulders.

She gasped softly at the first contact and her hands slid into his hair. Her musky feminine scent with a hint of chlorine surrounded him, drawing him closer. He lowered his lips to her neck. The taste of her skin was sweet and fresh.

His hands took a journey over smooth firm breasts. Beneath his palms he felt her hardened nipples. He rolled them between thumbs and forefingers, heard her whisper something as he closed his lips over one perfect bud.

'Touch me again, Blake.' Her voice had turned from teasing to seriously turned on. She shifted beneath his lips, lifting her hands to tug at pins and ribbons so that her hair fell loose and wet over her shoulders, a wildfire of curls. 'Come inside me.'

Her impatience urged him to take her now where they stood and his own need chafed at him but he would *not* be rushed.

Lifting his head, he slid his palms over her hips and let his gaze wander. Naked had never looked so perfect and he drank in the sight before him like a man too long between beers. He could feel the need radiating from her like a blush and lifted his gaze to hers.

Clear eyes stared back at him, drenched with desire, and

the air around her shimmered like the gold she'd dusted on her shoulders. His body burned with something more than lust. She was feminine perfection but she was still tiny. And she looked even smaller naked, and so fine-boned and fragile, as if she'd break with one touch.

'Don't think about whatever it is you're thinking about,' Lissa whispered, her heart racing as she leaned forward to place her lips on his chest. Circling his hard male nipples and learning their texture. Bending her head and discovering their taste—salt and sweet and...Blake.

He groaned with a sound that was part pleasure, part pain. 'You're exquisite,' he muttered with an almost savage growl. 'And, God...what I want to do with you...'

Twining her arms about his neck, she looked deep into his eyes. 'Glad to hear you still feel that way.'

And then he was sweeping her legs from beneath her and laying her on the softly damp grass. It was like falling endlessly into her dreams.

Silvery moonshine slanted across one sharp cheekbone as he stared down at her. Then darkness as his head blocked the light and his mouth closed over hers with a deep desperate kiss that told her he was as lost in the moment as she.

Her water-chilled, droplet-covered body all but steamed against the heat of his skin. She revelled in his rich, dark taste, her tongue sliding against his as she traced the hard planes of his shoulders with her fingertips, the bunched muscles of his upper arms. Loving the rasp of masculine hair against her breasts, her belly.

The hard hot length of his masculinity surged against her hip, but he made no move to use it. He lifted his head and watched his hand as he stroked a slow path from her neck and over one tingling nipple, then lower, to circle her navel with one feather-light fingertip. Her body arched instinctively against his touch like a flower searching for sunlight.

She held her breath… 'Oh, yes…' Finally, finally, oh… Her thighs fell open and she heard herself moan, closed her eyes and prepared to give herself up to the ultimate sensation for the second time in less than an hour.

'So hot,' he murmured as he opened her and pushed a finger inside her. 'So wet for me.'

His last possessive words and their simple truth squeezed at her heart. 'Yes,' she murmured back. *Only for you.*

Gentle. She'd never experienced such gentleness. She could feel the strength and the tension hum through his body and knew he was holding back. Unlike Todd who'd always raced to the finish without a thought for her needs. And unlike the man who'd betrayed her, she trusted Blake, wanted him to lose that control, wanted that heat and strength inside her. 'Blake…now.'

Eyes still closed, she trembled, poised on the thin edge between anticipation and something like fear. Fear that he'd stop.

He did. Then he swore, a strangled sound that had her opening her eyes. His expression was frozen. 'Protection.'

'I'm on the pill,' she gasped. 'I take care of my own.'

'My kind of girl,' he muttered and lowered himself slowly on top of her.

He slid inside her in one long smooth motion and her entire being quivered with the new intimacy. The pressure invaded her, expanding and radiating to every part of her body in a thousand glorious explosions and sending her hurtling towards climax.

The shock of the speed staggered her and she opened her eyes so she could see him, to know it was him inside her as she crested that stunning peak. His jaw was tight, his face almost grim with intensity as he watched her fly away.

'Blake,' she whispered. The tension spiralled then snapped

and she felt her limbs grow limp, sated. She'd been waiting her whole life for this moment. *Welcome home*.

But, oh…no… She couldn't let herself think that way. She'd told him herself that it was just sex. His home, and his *emotionless* life, were on the ocean.

Still…his eyes glittered like fire in the dimness as he moved inside her. And, at last, at long last, *she* was the woman who'd made them turn to indigo.

She was the woman whose hands skimmed that hot, taut skin, whose legs were wrapped around those powerful thighs as he plunged deeper, faster. She was the woman who arched against him as he found his own climax. He dropped down beside her and she cradled his head against her breast in the aftermath.

'Lissa…' Her name, murmured in that deep voice, curled around her like a sigh and told her more than he'd ever say.

So she could enjoy the masculine texture of his jaw against her breast a little while longer, she touched the side of his face and smiled to herself while the night's tiny wildlife rustled nearby. She could smell the fragrance of the new-mown grass, feel its soft scratchiness against her skin.

The sky was alive with stars, and, in the east, the waning moon on its ascent. Her life with all its twists and turns was suddenly, and for the moment at least, perfect.

He looked up at her, eyes searching hers. 'No regrets?'

'Not one.' She traced his eyebrows. 'You?'

He stroked a finger over her nipple, watched it pucker. 'You were amazing.'

Which didn't answer her question, but he was the master of evasion and she wasn't about to spoil it, especially when she felt him harden again against her hip. Already. 'It was pretty amazing, wasn't it?'

'So…' He leaned up on one elbow. His eyes were the colour of smoke and he smiled a wicked sailor's smile as he curled one hand around the back of her neck. 'What do you say we do it again? In a bed this time?'

'Or the pool.'

'I like the way you think.' He rose, sweeping her up with him and heading to the water. 'We've got all night. We can enjoy both.'

CHAPTER ELEVEN

YOU had to worship a man who brought you breakfast in bed on a silver tray after a night of carnal pleasure, especially if he was naked and built like a bronzed god. A bowl of fruit, poached eggs—hard—with toast and jam to follow. In addition to his pot of tea, he'd made her an instant coffee. She'd have preferred her early morning latté but he'd not familiarised himself with that piece of kitchen technology. And it wasn't early. It was well after midday.

'So what made you think I was a virgin?' she asked, around a mouthful of mango.

He grinned at her. 'Could be because you mentioned "after all this time" the first time I kissed you.'

She smiled, took another bite. 'That's because I'd only been waiting years and couldn't believe you were attracted to me.'

Blake leaned forward, licked the juice from her mouth. 'Believe it.' He smoothed her back and studied her. She wore the smile of a well-satisfied woman. 'You know, you have the most beautiful eyes I ever saw.' He hesitated. 'But sometimes…there's something there…like last night, when I hauled you into the bathroom at Gilda's.'

Her smile dropped away. 'I was surprised, that's all.'

He shook his head. 'Not all.'

Something didn't fit with her normally casual, easy-going

style. And he was absolutely, one-hundred-per-cent through seeing that startled, hunted look that stole into her eyes at odd times. All the more concerning when she was usually warm, willing and with him on so many levels.

A man, he was sure of it. 'What happened, Lissa? Who hurt you?'

'No one important.' Her eyes turned dull, flat. Distant.

A knot tightened in his chest. He touched her chin lightly and turned her head so she had no choice but to face him. 'What did he do? Tell me,' he demanded, when she didn't reply.

'I don't want to talk about it.'

'Would you rather I asked your brother?'

She stiffened, her eyes widening. 'You wouldn't.'

'If it helped, yes, I damn well would.'

'Jared doesn't know anything about him and I want to keep it that way.' She pushed his hand away. 'I'm not a kid and I don't need him or anyone else to fight my battles. He was a guy I met a year ago. Todd. We had a relationship.' Hesitation. 'An abusive relationship. He got a real kick out of seeing me scared.'

Anger didn't begin to describe what boiled up inside him as he looked at Lissa. So small and delicate. So vulnerable to the wrong sort. What cowardly scum got off on scaring a woman who'd put her trust in him? Worse, Lissa had called him abusive. What else had the low-life done?

Blake didn't need her to tell him. His imagination filled in the rest. 'The bastard.'

'That's what I told the cops. There was a restraining order. Haven't seen him for months. Last I heard he'd moved interstate.'

'You should've told Jared.'

She shook her head. 'No.'

'Yes.' He cupped her cheeks in both palms. 'Why the hell not?'

'Because I told you. We had a disagreement.' Her voice was clipped. Angry. Hurting. 'He's made a point of not coming here unless specifically invited ever since.' Her eyes filled with moisture. 'And there's a distance between us that was never there before.'

He tightened his fingers on her face. 'Ah, Lissa. He's your brother and he loves you. That'll never change.'

'I know,' she whispered, those tears spilling over.

Lissa covered his hands with hers on her cheeks, wanting to put this conversation away before she lost what was left of her composure. 'But the bad's in the past and I just want to move on. In lots of ways you've helped me do that. And the best thing you can do for me now is not to mention it again.

'You made me happy, Blake, last night and I hope I did the same for you. I haven't felt this good in a long long time. And it's not just the sex. It's you.'

'Lissa…'

She could almost hear his alarm bells ringing. 'It's okay,' she said quietly, drawing his hands away. 'You've been a true friend in my hour of need and you're already a great business partner, but sex does have a way of complicating things and we'll deal with it. The thing to remember is that you're not looking for an ongoing relationship and neither am I.'

Except this was Blake. The man she'd never got completely out of her thoughts. She picked up her coffee, stared into its depths. She wanted what they had for as long as it lasted and her heart was so going to pay for this later, but right now she couldn't see the thorns for the roses.

He was silent a moment, then nodded slowly. 'Let's take it one step at a time, then.' Darkly clouded eyes clashed with hers. Not the kind that wept soft rain but clouds that promised a cracking good lightning display, all light and heat and unleashed power.

'The business first,' he said. 'We should have a launch party. Get your name out there.'

'A party.' Taking his cue, she made a concerted effort to shake off the intensity of the last few moments. 'That's a brilliant idea. I've thought of a name. Lissa's Interior Design. Gilda— Oh-my-gosh...'

She grabbed her mobile, checked the time and sprang off the bed, spilling crumbs over the sheet. 'I arranged to be there in twenty minutes to check with her about the curtains. I'd better shower and get my act together.' She took a last look at the naked man ogling her bare butt as she slid through the doorway. 'Thank you, Blake. For every thing.'

Blake watched the pool's sunny reflections ripple across the ceiling. He'd been so relaxed last night he'd woken pain free from a dreamless sleep. In a bed that smelled of a warm, sated woman.

A woman who'd been used by a man in the worst possible way.

His fists tightened against the mattress. *Pond scum. Low-life.* He threw back the sheet and stalked to the window where he glared at the sun sparking off the river. Lissa wanted to forget and move on. So he'd not mention it again.

But he wouldn't forget.

He turned from the view and, in an automatic move, picked up his clothes from the floor, folded them and set them on a chair. And what of Blake Everett? Was he any more worthy of someone like her? He was a wanderer. A loner. A lasting relationship for him and someone like Lissa, or anyone else for that matter, was never going to happen. Home and family weren't in his destiny.

Lissa, on the other hand, needed that security, that bond of family. If there was one thing he could do for Lissa before he left, it would be to get some open and honest conversation between her and Jared happening again.

She'd told him she wasn't looking for an ongoing relationship and he could understand why she might feel that way at present. But given time to heal, that might change.

Whereas for them…they'd had great sex. Mutually satisfying sex.

And mutually satisfying sex was all it was. All it could be. He refused to acknowledge anything more. He'd been cruising through life just fine on his own. Okay, his ship-mates were as close as family and navy life offered little privacy, but on shore leave or one of his rare recreational night dives—in the quiet, solitary times he'd found peace. Or close to it.

Until last month.

His bare toes connected with the brass bed base and pain ricocheted up his shin and he swore like the sailor he was. Yeah, he thought almost savagely, Lissa, with her sheltered upbringing, knew nothing of the murky depths beneath the surface of his civilian persona. She'd never understand the trauma of watching someone dying before her eyes and to wake up and know there'd been nothing she could have done to stop it.

And yet she'd offered him comfort when he'd woken downstairs the other night. She'd listened. Really listened. She'd talked—sensibly, with maturity and sensitivity—about posttraumatic stress. He'd been the one to cut off the communication because he still refused to believe that was what he suffered from. *Never reveal your weaknesses.*

He stared down at the place where they'd made love. Last night, lying beside her, he'd felt something he'd never experienced. Something warm, something worthwhile, like… trust?

Jaw tightening, he turned away. *No.* His father had wanted nothing to do with him. His mother had been trusted to put on a good benefit show, but when it had come to her only son, she'd fallen far short. That innate trust in the love and comfort of family had been wiped clean at an early age.

He thought of Janine. He'd fallen for her hook, line and

sinker. He'd ripped out his scarred heart and laid it at her feet and she'd crushed it beneath her heel with her lies and betrayal.

So much for trust. He would never lay himself on the line that way for anyone, ever again.

He stalked to the bathroom and had just switched on the spray when his mobile buzzed on the bedside table. He switched the water off again, swiped a towel from the rail and went to answer it. Jared's familiar voice caught him off guard.

'Hey. What are you doing up so early?' Blake turned from the sight of sex-rumpled sheets and one of Lissa's gold hair ribbons and moved away from the bed. The last person he wanted to talk to with the scent of Lissa on his body was her big brother. 'What time is it there?'

'A tick before the crack of dawn. Isaac's an early riser.' Blake heard a muffled sound then a distant, 'Hey buddy, put that down, Mummy'll have my b— Isaac...' A crash. 'Never mind, I'll buy her another one.' He sounded resigned, then spoke into the phone again. 'You still there?'

'Still here. Kids, eh?'

'Yeah. Who'd have 'em?'

But Blake heard an exuberance of love in his mate's voice. 'I bet he's a firecracker.'

'You got that right.' There was a hesitation through the phone, then Jared's voice turned serious. 'Before I speak to Lissa, I've been talking to Soph and we're wondering if we should cut short our trip and come home.'

And wouldn't that throw everything into a spin?

No mention of the business, Blake noted, and cleared his throat. Damn it. Lissa obviously hadn't contacted him herself yet. 'She hasn't called?'

'No. And her phone's been switched off for hours.'

'We were at a party till late—'

'You and Liss...?'

He heard the surprise in his old mate's voice. 'Yeah.' *Moving right along.* 'She's next door at the moment, doing up a quote for a nursery. I'll get her to call you when she comes back.'

'So she's getting some work. That's one good thing I suppose. How's she taking the boat disaster, do you think?'

'She's doing okay. Still a little shocked but—'

'Not enough to prevent her from partying obviously.'

'It was a charity thing,' Blake felt obliged to point out in her defence.

'She wants to start her own business. It concerns me a lot. I don't think she's ready for it. Has she mentioned anything about that to you? I guess she's got enough to think about right now.'

Blake paced the carpet, feeling as if he were sinking further into quicksand with every step he took. Yet here was an opportunity to get them talking. 'I'll let her tell you about it.'

'I was hoping to hear your opinion.'

Blake really didn't want to get into anything serious here after doing the wild thing with her all night. 'Better coming from her, mate,' he said, scrubbing a hand down his face. 'She'll call as soon as she gets in.'

'Blake…we were buddies a long while. Is there something I should know here?'

Hell. His grip tightened on the phone. He couldn't talk about their business arrangement because he'd given his word to Lissa, even though he knew that wasn't what his mate was asking. 'She's an adult, Jared. She makes her own decisions.'

Silence. 'What the hell's that supposed to mean?'

'Like I said, she'll tell you herself.'

'So there *is* something going on.'

'At ease, mate, nothing to be alarmed about.'

'She's my sister. I don't want to see her hurt.' There was an edge to his voice that could slice through steel.

'Nor do I.'

'Tell her to call me via webcam. I want to see how she's taking this—and whatever else—for myself.'

'No worries. The moment she's back.'

Jared disconnected without another word.

Blake stared at the dead phone. 'That went well,' he muttered, and headed back to the bathroom to take his shower.

He thought about Jared's concern as he put his room back into some kind of order. Despite her pride in her independence, Lissa was a family girl at heart. She'd probably tire of her party ways eventually and settle down. Marry an easy-going Mr Joe-Average Nice-Guy with no emotional baggage and have two stunning kids, a boisterous dog and a comfortable four-bedroom home overlooking the beach.

Not for him. It was time to look at purchasing his own boat. Time to get moving, explore all the dives along the coast. Use the stars as his compass and live the dream before it was too late. Wasn't that what it was all about?

He collected Lissa's ribbons and hairpins and took them down the hall, but stopped in her bedroom doorway. Was there a bed somewhere beneath those shopping bags? How did someone who'd just lost everything manage to accumulate such a chaos in a single day?

The en-suite fared no better. Lotions of every description and bottles with tops off littered the vanity. A wet towel trailed from the basin. He left her ribbons beside her hairbrush and screwed the lid back on the toothpaste. Another reason they'd never work out. He liked his life ordered. He liked his space clear. She'd drive him crazy.

What they had was just temporary, he assured himself again as he walked away. A fling. She'd drive someone else crazy some day.

CHAPTER TWELVE

SHE'D drive someone else crazy some day.

Blake needed something else to take his mind off the persistent and distracting thought rattling around in his head. Problem was, his day's routine was shot. He'd not had his morning run—he'd been 'otherwise occupied'. And now the afternoon was slipping away and Lissa was still busy with Gilda. Probably catching up on last night's success. He needed a diversion.

Food. He'd cook something for dinner. How long since he'd enjoyed a good home-cooked meal? He checked the pantry supplies, began compiling a list, then stopped. He had no idea what Lissa liked. Still, who'd not enjoy a good old-fashioned Aussie lamb roast? It could cook while he…what?

Waited for Lissa to come home?

The scene played before his eyes:

He's just put the finishing touches on a complicated dish that took all afternoon to prepare. The leafy salad with a new mustard/pepper dressing is chilling in the fridge along with a bottle of chardonnay. He's thinking cheese for afters, with a little quince pâté, some grapes…then a leisurely bubble bath and an early night…

Lissa rushes through the door, her blouse askew, her hair dishevelled from driving the convertible with the top down. Dinner meeting—sorry, did she forget to tell him? She fishes a couple of cherry tomatoes from the salad bowl in the fridge then a peck on his cheek on her way past. Don't wait up, it's going to be a long one—some after-dinner function to attend and, oh, would he mind collecting her dry cleaning before the shop closes?

Blake stumbled back a step, scowling. What the hell had happened to that bubble bath? What—

'I'm back,' Lissa sang out as she danced into the kitchen, her face glowing, her hair flying behind her. 'Oh, you should see how the nursery's coming along.' She did a quick twirl. 'It's going to be stunning. And she loves the colours. And Gilda's offered to make it a glittering affair with all her rich friends and Stefan's going to take pictures for the PowerPoint presentation at the launch and everyone will see it…and… Hi.' She exhaled hugely on the final word and smiled like sunshine.

Blake blinked, feeling as if he'd just been flattened by a runaway lawnmower. 'Hi.' He screwed up his shopping list, tossed it on the sink. She was wearing a lettuce-green sundress with cherries on and tomato sauce spaghetti straps. Damn the roast, he wanted to take her on the nearest available surface and feed on her instead.

But the domestic role-reversal scene continued to shimmer dangerously before his eyes. Damned if she was going to leave him home alone all night while she got up to…whatever.

Her smile faded a little. 'You could sound more enthusiastic, it's your business too.'

'You're enthusiastic enough for both of us.' With an effort, he snapped himself back to the present and the vision of delightedness before him. She was here now, and for now she was all his. He pushed the uneasiness aside. 'Come here.'

She stepped unhesitatingly into his embrace with the ease and comfort of a familiar lover, linked her arms around his neck and tilted her head up, her lips a breath away from his. 'Have you any idea how I feel right now?'

'Yeah.' He smoothed his hands over her shoulders beneath the straps of her sundress and pressed his mouth against her neck. Impossible not to linger a moment, to feast on that almost translucent skin. 'Oh, yeah.' He lifted his head to watch her face as he ran his hands down her sides—the dip of her waist, the flare of her hips beneath skin-scented cotton. 'You feel incredible. Good enough to eat, in fact.' Lowering his lips, he rubbed them lightly over hers and tasted the faint bitterness of coffee, the stronger, sweeter hint of vanilla and almonds. He flicked his tongue out, sampled the corner of her mouth where the flavour was more delicate. 'Gilda's been feeding you.'

'Mmm.' She wriggled closer, tightened her hold and her breasts rubbed against his chest. 'But I'm still hungry.' She opened her mouth, took his lower lip between her teeth and bit down. 'So hungry...' she soothed the tingle with her tongue, then sucked gently '...I could eat you too.'

He lifted her off the floor and she clamped her thighs around his waist, her eyes hot, her rose-bud lips parted. His blood thundered in his ears and hammered in his groin.

'Yeah. Who needs a lamb roast?' he murmured against her mouth as his fingers clenched around her bottom, bringing her intimate heat into contact with his belly.

His gaze remained fused with hers as he carried her to the kitchen island, set her on the edge of the smooth marble and pushed her thighs apart. Then he braced his hands on the counter top and leaned in while she twisted her fingers in his T-shirt, knuckles white, pressed against his chest.

Falling into the kiss was like leaping out of a plane and into the clouds. Fast and exhilarating, destination uncertain. And for the moment he didn't care. The journey was enough.

The skinny strip of white lace was no barrier—a flick of his wrist, a quick tug and it was gone. Freeing himself, he plunged inside her. He heard her gasp; her eyes were wide and dark as he withdrew slowly. Plunged again. Harder, deeper. Faster.

He feasted on her sweet taste, swallowed her sighs as she met him beat for beat with an enthusiasm that rivalled his. They gorged on each other with mouths and tongues and teeth, the past forgotten, the future unclear.

She surrounded him, slick heat and damp, dark desire, the tight liquid tug pulling him towards completion too fast. Way too fast. The notion that he was *here at last* registered vaguely on some distant horizon.

Then no words, no time, no thought, just a fierce, fast, furious coupling. The need to possess her, a demand to drive reason from her mind so that he was all she knew— all he knew—hammered through his mind in time with his thrusts.

Lissa had never known such a frenzy of wants and desires, needs and demands. Her hands rushed beneath his T-shirt to find all those hard muscles beneath damp skin. He didn't try to hold her or pin her down in any way and rational thought fled as she gave herself up to the whirlwind of sensations battering her. And, oh, how liberating to allow herself to be swept along in its wake, knowing she was safe, that she'd found a haven in Blake.

And somewhere amidst the maelstrom she found the eye of the storm, the calm, her centre.

She held tight to it as they raced together to the finish.

Moments later she slid her hands from beneath the soft cotton tee to wrap them around his forearms braced either side of her. Her thighs trembled, her whole body was limp and tiny exquisite aftershocks still shuddered through her body.

'Lissa.' Breathing heavily, he looked into her eyes and she saw a glimmer of concern. 'I'll replace the underwear.'

If that was all that was bothering him… She opened her mouth to answer and discovered her throat was dry. This new physical facet of their relationship was moving at warp speed and she was still trying to catch up.

But emotionally, Lissa knew she was light-years ahead. He would *not* want to know she was falling in love with him.

'Lissa?' He lifted her chin with a finger, searching her eyes. And she knew he was remembering their earlier conversation about no complications. No ongoing relationship.

She leaned forward, pressed a quick kiss on his lips. 'No need. Thanks to you I have a whole new drawer full of undies,' she assured him, swallowing the ball of emotion that had rolled up her throat. 'And it was so worth it.' *Sunny but casual.* 'That was...*fa-a-a*-n-tastic.' She stretched her arms, let them relax onto his shoulders and smiled. How could she not? She'd just been ravished on a kitchen counter. 'Did I hear a lamb roast mentioned somewhere?'

His smile was...smug? 'Too late to start now but I can do tuna cakes with a side salad.'

'And he cooks too,' she murmured, and kissed him lightly on the lips. 'I'll make the salad.'

'No.' He slid her off the counter and deposited her on the floor. His smile disappeared. 'You'll call Jared. He phoned while you were gone.'

Oh. 'Right.' She heard the message in Blake's tone. She should have made that call earlier. 'I take it you didn't tell him about the business?'

'That's your task.' He walked to the fridge and began pulling out ingredients. 'He asked you to call him via webcam. He wants to see how you are for himself.'

With the satisfied glow of love-making in her eyes? Not flipping likely. 'Oh, *bother*—the computer's down, right?' And her phone was too old for image-to-image capabilities.

'I guess it is.' He glanced at her as he set a bowl and chopping board on the counter where she'd been sitting moments ago. She felt herself colour. She'd never look at that counter in the same way again.

Taking her phone outside, she settled herself on a lounger by the pool in the fading afternoon's warmth and called Jared. She started with an apology, briefly summarised what had been happening with the boat, then talked to little Isaac a moment, which gave her time to psych herself up for the next round of information.

'Blake and I have gone into business together.' As quick and easy as that, she thought.

'I see.'

Clearly he didn't.

She lay back and watched the palm fronds move in the breeze and told herself not to overreact. 'He didn't tell you because I asked him not to. I wanted to do it myself. Just listen first, will you?'

She hurried on with a quick overview, then outlined the details of her new partnership with Blake, his living-room makeover clause, the new clients she'd got and how fortunate she was to be getting her own business ra, ra, ra.

'So, it makes sense to stay at Blake's for now,' she finished.

Silence.

She tracked the calming sight of flight of a flock of water birds as they skimmed the water. *Calm, calm, calm.*

'Is that wise, Liss?'

Calm vanished and irritation prickled between her shoulder blades but she kept her voice steady. 'What are you implying?' She flicked at an insect on her dress with a fingernail, then tapped on the lounger's metal arm. 'You know Blake—it's not as if he's a stranger.'

'I know you had a little crush on him as a teenager but he's been in the navy for fourteen years apart from that brief trip home when his mother died. He's a sailor, for God's sake.'

'A clearance diver, to be precise.' *Jared knew about her crush?* Her calm slipped another notch. 'The naval equivalent to the Special Air Services.'

'So he informed me,' he replied coolly. 'I *am* aware of what they do, Lissa.'

'At least you know he's not just any guy I picked up at a party.' Like Todd.

'Are you sleeping with him?'

She jerked upright. Forget calm, forget irritated, *now* she was angry. 'Is that *any* of your business?'

'My God, you are. It's been what…days?'

'Careful, Jared. Glass houses.' She fought for composure; she didn't want to argue long-distance.

There was a long pause. 'He's not going to hang around for long, honey. He's buying himself a boat. Are you prepared for that?'

She knew. And she'd never be prepared. The heartache would come and the knowledge stabbed at her. She wished she'd thought to bring a drink with her to wash away the dry taste in her mouth. 'I know all that. I'm not a kid.'

'A man like Blake is not the settling-in-one-place kind of guy. He—'

'Oh, for heaven's sakes, didn't you ever have a fling in your life? One wild, crazy no-strings affair with no unrealistic expectations?' Then she frowned, remembering he'd been too busy being a parent to her, and said quietly, 'No, I guess you didn't.'

'Is that what this is?'

She blinked back a sudden moisture, already storing memories of Blake in her heart. 'What else would it be?' What else *could* it be? She gave a light laugh for Jared's benefit, but it came out loud, brittle and over-bright. 'You know me. Always busy. Too busy for anything more and that's not going to change any time soon.' *The world's worst fibber.* 'Don't worry, he'll be gone and it'll be over before you know it.'

'What about the business?' he said. 'I hope you—'

'Of course. Priority number one, but, as I used to tell you often enough, all work and no play…'

'Just…look after yourself.'

'Always.'

'We love you.' Gruff and stern. Not happy. Not happy at all.

'Love you too.' She did. She really did. But she forced a sunny-as-you-go smile into her voice. 'Bye for now.'

She disconnected, leaned back and closed her eyes, moisture clinging to her lashes. Let him get used to the idea. No surprises when he came home from overseas.

Blake might already be gone by then.

Relax. Breathe. Don't let Blake see you like this.

So while she got her emotions under control she reminded herself of the conversation and why she needed to listen to her head and not her heart. She didn't need Jared to tell her Blake wasn't the right man for her. Not long term.

She'd want too much from him—already wanted too much—and an ongoing relationship with a man who lived a million miles away on a boat just wouldn't work. It was vital for her own well-being that she accepted their liaison for what it was and lived the next few weeks accordingly.

A short-term affair.

Blake leaned a shoulder against the open doorway and watched Lissa through narrowed eyes. He couldn't see her face from this angle but she'd disconnected and stretched out as if she didn't have a care in the world.

He'd been about to step outside when he'd heard her spill the status of their relationship to her brother.

He'll be gone and it'll be over before you know it. He'd seen the flip of her hand as she said it. Chuckled it even.

Amused and casual about it all, was she? She'd been anything but amused and casual last night, he remembered darkly.

She'd told it how it was—fun and games for as long as it lasted. *A wild, crazy no-strings affair,* he'd heard her tell Jared.

That was what Blake wanted too, he told himself. And what better way to de-stress than a fling with a gorgeous, fun-loving woman who knew where they stood? It had always worked before.

So why did he feel as if he'd been trussed with barbed wire and tossed overboard into a storm-ravaged sea?

He was a navy man, he reminded himself. He knew how to swim. Tension coiling through every muscle in his body, he pushed off the door frame. 'Food's cooked,' he said. 'You about ready to eat?'

She jumped at his voice and scrambled upright. 'Sure am.' Facing away from him, deliberately, he guessed, she rose, all loose-limbed grace, and stared at the tangerine-smeared sky. 'I never tire of this view.'

'Me neither,' he agreed, willing to stand there for however long it took and watch her with the balmy breeze carrying her scent to his nose and the languid sound of a clarinet drifting from a house across the river.

Then she turned and she was smiling and the force of it hit him smack in the chest. He rubbed a hand over the tender spot, then said, 'I'll miss it when I go.'

Her smile remained but something in her eyes changed. His words had hit their intended target and he wished he'd kept his mouth shut. He wished he knew what she was feeling.

He wished to hell he knew if he was the only one suffering the same gut-rending, devastating force that held him motionless.

Rubbing her upper arms, she glanced away over her shoulder, as if a chill were stalking her. 'It's gorgeous outside. Why don't we eat by the pool?'

They shared a bottle of white wine with their meal as the violet dusk settled into night and the insects chittered. He lit the tea candles he'd brought out with them so he could enjoy the way the light glinted on the gold highlights in her auburn hair.

He didn't pay much attention to their conversation. He was too distracted by the sound of her voice and the way her hands moved as she talked and his own thoughts racing inside his head.

Until she said, 'Gilda was telling me how you saved her life. She had other good things to say about you too.'

Thanks a lot, Gil. What he didn't need right now was to have his life dissected, however well intentioned. The less Lissa knew, the less involved she'd be when he left. 'I just did what anyone would have done.'

She spread her hands on the table. 'I guess you've saved a lot of lives over your time in the navy.'

He shifted, uncomfortable with the conversation, and poured himself another glass of wine, drank half of it straight down. 'It goes with the job.'

'And do you—did you—like your job?'

'It has its moments.' He'd been thinking a lot about that over the past couple of weeks. He'd reached his personal horizon as far as the navy was concerned. It had been time to leave and plot a new course for his life.

'So why did you join the navy?'

'I always loved the sea. Its vastness. The solitude.'

'Solitude? In a navy vessel?' She grinned.

'Yeah, okay, you got me there.'

'I still remember when you left. Here one day, gone the next.'

He shook his head. 'Not quite but it might have seemed that way.'

'Heartbreaker,' she murmured. 'I cried for a week.'

He stared at her, remembering the young teenager and felt…odd. He was still uncomfortable by the whole idea that she'd more than likely projected her sexual fantasies onto him, a guy nine years her senior. 'You did not.'

She lifted a shoulder. 'Okay, maybe it was only a couple

of days, but I might have if I... Not after... Never mind,' she finished quietly. 'It's not important.'

And as if Lissa had conjured her up, an image of Janine shimmered in front of his eyes. The Ghost of Mistakes Past. His mood darkened. 'Don't stop now, it's just getting interesting.' He drained his glass, leaned back and gestured for her to continue.

She was silent a moment, then said, 'Okay. I'm not going to pretend I didn't hear the rumours.' Her voice was as soft as the evening air.

'Why would you?'

'To spare you pain...or embarrassment maybe?'

He shook his head. Not pain, not any more. He'd taught himself not to react every time he thought of Janine. Not embarrassment because he didn't give a rat's ass what others thought they knew. 'Don't spare my feelings, Lissa. Either you believe the gossip-mongers or you don't.' Watching her, he reached for the wine bottle, raised it to his lips but didn't drink.

'I didn't really know you back then. You weren't real. You were more a...fantasy.' She looked down at her hands, then back at him. 'But I'm beginning to know the man you are now. You're kind and generous, you're a good listener, you care about others—'

'But you don't know whether to believe the rumours or not.'

She lifted her glass, sipped from it, set it down again. 'Of course I don't believe them.'

Was she telling the truth about how she felt? Or was it a carefully disguised attempt? He realised that what she thought mattered to him a great deal more than he'd have liked.

'You can't decide,' he said, watching her. 'You want to believe they're lies but deep down inside you, there's always been that doubt. Who is Blake Everett? Not the man you wanted to see, but the real man? Could he make a girl pregnant then walk away? Could he walk away from his own child?'

'Stop it, Blake.'

'And now we've had sex, you think a bit further…and you wonder, what if, just once, your pills don't work? You ask yourself, 'Would he walk away from me? Would he leave me to raise our child alone?''

She shook her head, closed her eyes. 'Stop.'

'Maybe I could walk away. Maybe my upbringing convinced me that alone was best, that responsibility didn't matter.' He turned the bottle in his hands, studying the distorted image of the burning candle through the glass. Everyone had their own way of looking at things.

'Or perhaps back then, I simply made the problem go away. Don't tell me that never crossed your mind.' He looked into her eyes, read the answer.

'Blake, please, I know you better now.'

He picked up her glass, downed the rest of her wine in one long swallow and said, 'Let me tell you about Janine.'

CHAPTER THIRTEEN

'You don't have to. I know you'd never do what they say you did.'

He challenged her clear-eyed gaze. 'Maybe I want to set the record straight.' *For you at least.* He cared more than he wanted to what Lissa believed and what she thought about him.

He looked up, away from the warm distraction before him, to the cold blue emotionless stars. 'I met Janine at the beach. She asked me about life-saving. Said she was interested in joining. She lived in a small apartment on the edge of town and was studying law and pulling late-night shifts at a nearby club to pay her fees.

'Her body was every teenage guy's fantasy but she didn't even seem to be aware of it. She had a freshness about her and a keen mind and I found the combination irresistible.

'We started dating. I saw her every day for lunch and in the evening before she had to go to work. We were together for two months. The houseboat didn't feel right so I told her I intended getting us a bigger place and supporting her so she didn't have to work nights. I'd already bought and sold my first property and was making a reasonable income at the dive shop.

'But before we'd met I'd arranged to sail from Perth to Port Lincoln. I wanted to test my sea legs and the Great Australian

Bight has some of the world's roughest seas. Throw in some scuba diving and I was supposed to be gone five weeks. She cried all over me the day before I left and told me how much she loved me and how she couldn't bear to be without me. I cut my journey short by ten days for her.

'Then a week later she told me she was pregnant and that we needed to get married fast. I hadn't known who her parents were until then. She'd kept very quiet about her privileged upbringing.'

Lissa frowned, doing the calculations. 'How pregnant?'

Exactly. 'She didn't say and it didn't occur to me to ask. She said it didn't matter since we loved each other and I'd forget the navy now we had a baby on the way.' He blew out a breath. The old pain still had the ability to crush. 'You know, she nearly had me. Then I saw her due date on a report she'd carelessly left inside a pregnancy advice book on her bedside table. There was no way I could have been the father.'

He'd been devastated. He'd let himself be drawn into love only to be betrayed again. *It had been the last time.*

He jerked himself out of the memory. 'So I did some quick investigating. Turned out her night shifts hadn't been of the waitressing kind. I went to Sydney and joined the navy a week later.'

'How could someone do that?' Lissa's voice seemed to come from a long way away.

'Quite easily, it would seem.'

'Blake, I'm…' Lissa swallowed. He wouldn't want her pity. 'That must have been tough.' She reached out and covered his hand with hers on the table and felt him flinch.

Before she could think of how to tell him she understood his anguish, she stopped. Because she *didn't* understand. She had no idea how he felt. Whether he'd have given up his navy dreams to be a father. To make a home with her and the baby.

He pulled his hand away, flexed it at his side and rose abruptly. 'I'm going for a run.'

Lissa's heart ached on his behalf. She'd tried reaching out and he'd rejected that, so she just said, 'Take care,' as he stalked away.

There was a coolness in the air and it wasn't just the evening's breeze from the river. Janine's deception had broken something inside Blake and talking about it tonight had scraped at the old wounds. She knew he needed that alone time.

She cleared the dishes, hoping Blake would come back soon and she could see how he was. When he didn't, she went to the room where she'd set up her artwork. She pushed the window wide to let in the evening.

Ears strained, she listened for the sound of Blake's footsteps on the pavement. She could hear nature's soft night music, the distant sounds of a party in progress. The frangipani's scent from outside mingled with the tang of turpentine and charcoal.

With a sigh, she tucked her legs beneath her on the tarpaulin she'd set on top of the carpet, letting her gaze meander through the window to the river with the spill of moonlight shimmering like pearl beads on black velvet.

The moonlit scene reminded her that she loved working with black and white. She opened her sketch pad. If only problems were as clear-cut. She selected a black pencil with a blunt smudged tip and drifted it at random over the blank page.

She wasn't aware of time or her cramped fingers or the moon's slow arc across the sky. Nothing took her attention from her work. Until she felt the hairs on her neck rise.

For a few seconds she froze, remembering how Todd used to creep up on her, finding it funny to see her jump.

She looked over her shoulder. And her heart started beating again...*Blake*.

'I startled you.'

'Only a bit. I'm all right.'

He watched her a moment without speaking.

'You okay?' she asked.

He barely nodded.

No words could describe the moment. The way he looked at her. The way she felt. No words necessary as he crossed the room and stretched out behind her on the tarp. No words spoken as she turned and slid down beside him.

They undressed each other with only the sounds of their breathing and the whisper of clothing being shed in the silence. Slow in the intimacy of night's darkness, skin slid against skin. Heart beat against heart. Fingers entwined. Mouths coming together, clinging a moment then moving on to sip and soothe.

And Lissa knew, with every touch, every murmur, every lingering look, that this understanding could only be forged from love.

If only he knew it too.

Over the next couple of weeks, Lissa barely had time to turn around. Gilda's nursery was finished, photographed and filed for future reference. It was a magical 'Cinderella meets Snow White' theme with a pumpkin-shaped crib and a fortune in fabrics and fittings. Blake praised the new-look living room with its deep turquoise walls and mustard and dark gold furnishings. Another nursery was completed for a client she'd met at Gilda's party. Primrose walls, clean white furniture and a black lacquered crib for the central focus.

The rest of the furniture for the shop arrived. Spacious sofas, unique lamps, wallpaper hangings for customers to browse and office supplies. All were pulled together with the use of vivid colours and hours of hard slog.

They worked as a team. Blake handled the finances, any purchases needed and worked with an IT tech to build a website. When she wasn't trawling catalogues and home-living stores, Lissa was visiting clients, sketching ideas, giving quotes and working on the publicity for the upcoming launch.

But at night they fell asleep together. There were some days when those few precious hours were the only time they saw each other and Lissa grew accustomed to waking with someone beside her again.

She'd learned to read Blake's pain. She was happy to note that he'd only had one headache since that first time she'd found him on the couch. He'd needed the break to recover. If only he would come clean about his military past. He'd done his duty for his country and it was time he tried something else, even if it took him away from her.

Lissa knew he wasn't going to be around for ever. The business was her dream, not his. As if to reinforce that point he'd gone to Surfers one day to look at boats. He'd come home with a renewed enthusiasm...and it scared her.

Requests for work came in, thanks to Gilda's abundantly wealthy friends. Blake had suggested it might be time to start looking for a suitable part-time employee. 'You don't want to lose business because you can't keep up the pace.'

Because he wasn't going to be here to help, she thought, and another piece of her heart broke. The reality was, he'd never said he would be and he'd been up front about it from day one. Silent partner.

The night before the big event, they celebrated their hard-won achievements with oysters, Thai fish cakes and French champagne beneath the white shade sails of an open-air restaurant on the esplanade and watched the night-darkened waves lap the shoreline. Then they took off their shoes and strolled along the beach, which was still populated with tourists and locals alike enjoying the warm evening before heading home.

When they arrived back at the house, Blake kissed Lissa the moment he switched off the car's ignition. A long, deep kiss that reached right down to her toes and left her breathless and had every cell in her body clamouring for more.

'I've wanted to do that all evening,' Blake murmured when he at last lifted his head.

'And I've been waiting for it all evening too.'

His gaze darkened within the car's confines and dropped to her tingling lips. 'Have you now?'

'Seems like for ever. I have to tell you I can't wait much longer...' Feeling bolder than she had in a long, long time, she reached across and rubbed her hand over his crotch. She watched him harden against her fingers and felt its heat reflected in her cheeks as she looked up at him. 'Obviously you can't either.'

Humour danced around his mouth as he yanked the car key from the ignition and their gazes locked. 'And who's responsible for that?'

Still watching him, she pulled her house key from her purse. 'Race you to the bedroom.' She swung open the door and was out of the car like a rabbit. She laughed when she heard Blake swear, kicked off her shoes and kept running, urgency skipping through her veins.

He'd gained ground by the time she'd unlocked the door and pushed inside. Just behind her on the stairs. She screamed when she felt his fingers touch her hair and threw herself onto the bed. 'I won.' She let out a slightly inebriated whoop and flopped back onto the quilt.

'I was at a disadvantage.' He flicked on the bedside lamp, filling the room with a warm glow.

'No.' Out of breath, she stared up at him and bit her lip to stop the smile. 'You have longer legs.'

She watched him whip off his belt, slide it through his fingers. His eyes turned to smoke, the humour faded, replaced by an intensity she'd never seen before, and a sliver of uncertainty shimmied down her spine.

Her pulse stuttered, but not in a good way. 'Okay, call it a draw. It's over.'

'It's only just beginning,' Blake told her, and followed her down.

In a lightning move she wasn't prepared for, he grasped both her wrists, propelled them above her head as his mouth swooped on hers. The weight of his body pushed her into the mattress, one rock hard thigh pushed her legs apart.

Her heart pounded in her ears. She couldn't get enough air. She couldn't *breathe*.

But the instant she tried to pull her hands free, his hold loosened. 'Lissa?'

She dragged in a much needed breath. 'It's okay. I'm okay.'

Guilt steamed through Blake. What the hell had he been thinking, going at her that way after what she'd told him? He knew she didn't want to talk about it so, without a word, he leaned down and kissed her. Then he rolled over, bringing her on top of him.

Her hair fell in a curtain, cocooning both of them in its fresh fruity fragrance. He soothed her back with light strokes for a few moments, then kissed her shoulder and said, 'How about you doing all the work this time?'

'Me?' she murmured against his chest.

'I don't see anyone else here.'

She lay so still he wondered if he'd got it wrong but then she stirred. A slow sinuous movement that made his toes curl and his stomach muscles spasm as she pressed her lips to his chest and stretched. 'Hmm. If you insist. But it has to be my way all the way.'

He jerked when she scratched his nipples with the tips of her fingernails. 'Your way, sweet cheeks. I'm waiting…'

She sat up, her thighs gripping his hips, the hem of her loose-fitting dress sliding up to her waist. Wordlessly, she began undoing his shirt buttons. When she'd finished that task she pushed the fabric aside and smoothed her hands over his chest, her eyes clear now, and focused, and he breathed a sigh—part relief, part pain, but mostly he was just plain hot.

Lissa looked into his eyes and wished she could tell him what he'd done for her with his one simple suggestion that showed he understood. He'd given her her soul back, this man.

This man she loved.

Her heart both swelled and wept. She'd been so stupid. She'd fallen into the trap she'd told herself to steer well clear of. And he'd warned her, hadn't he? He'd been up front with her from day one. He was a sailor, he had a life and he didn't want to share it. With her unrealistic romantic fantasies, she only had herself to blame.

So no tears. And above all, no regrets.

'Jeez, woman, you're killing me here.'

His edgy demand brought her back to the present, and that was about all she had left. 'Patience,' she told him.

He reached for her hem but she batted his hand away. 'No.' She did it herself, lifting it up, throwing it to the floor. And, oh, the rush of feminine empowerment as she reached behind her back to unsnap her bra and toss it behind her.

He eyed her bare breasts with barely restrained hunger but she shook her head. 'No touching. Not yet.' Then she leaned back and took her weight on her hands and ordered him to, 'Take off your shirt.'

A difficult task, she conceded, since she was sitting on the tops of his thighs, but he managed to free his arms. He stuck them behind his head and lay back to await further instructions.

What freedom. What joy. What delight to have this man at

her mercy beneath her. 'You know, I used to fantasise about doing this,' she told him, and watched his eyelashes flicker.

'I don't think I needed to know that,' he murmured, his voice thick.

'Then I won't tell you what else I imagined…' She slanted off him to one side and gestured at his crotch. 'Now the pants. Then hands back behind your head.'

When the clothing was gone and he'd resumed his semi-relaxed pose, she moved back on top of him. She took him in her hands and slowly slid herself down his length. 'Ooh, that feels so good…'

She raised herself up, sank again and he thrust his hips to meet her, pushing further inside. Slow and slick and slippery. Watching his face now, she ran her hands through her hair, relishing the moment as they moved together. Glorying in the final rush to fulfilment.

Moments later she slid off to one side and stretched, before flopping an arm over Blake's chest and cuddling into his side.

'So…tomorrow's the big day,' he said, lifting her hand and rubbing her palm with his thumb.

'I wish Jared could've made it but he's been held up in Singapore with work. He was *supposed* to be on vacation.'

Blake brought her fingers to his lips and kissed each of them in turn. 'Crystal and Ian are coming.'

'Yes.'

But he knew it was Jared she wanted to see. At least they were talking more and, from what she'd told him, Jared sounded happy with the way the business was shaping up. 'He'll be there in spirit.'

'I know.'

'You still haven't told me what charity you're raising money for.'

'It's a surprise. Only Gilda knows.'

'I'm not a big fan of surprises.'

'Then toughen up, big boy, because I'm not telling you. You'll find out tomorrow like everyone else. Now go to sleep.'

He was back on the beach that haunted his dreams. But this time he found himself suspended in mid-air, looking down. Torque was gone, Lissa stood on the sand instead. The breeze caught her hair, twirling it about her beautiful face, which was turned towards the sun. She looked up, smiled at him, waved, then set off down the blinding strip. His heart stuttered. He wanted to wave back, tell her he was coming and ask her to wait but he couldn't move his arm.

And then she was sinking into the sand, her face contorted in horror as she screamed his name, over and over. He tumbled down to earth and onto the beach and started running but his legs were columns of concrete. Then the world turned dark as he pin-wheeled towards a rocky outcrop on the water's edge…

'Blake. Blake, you're having a bad dream.'

Lissa. Not screaming. Her soothing voice washed over him. He felt her hand on his chest and opened his eyes to see her leaning over him, her silhouette outlined against the grey light from the window. He could just make out her features in the darkness. Eyes wide and filled with something akin to the fear that still ripped through his body.

He'd not had his nightmare for weeks. He'd thought they were gone. But this dream was different. His subconscious was warning him to stay away from her, to keep her safe from him and harm.

'You're not going to shut me out any longer,' she said firmly. 'And you're not the only one who reads eyes.'

He turned his head away on the pillow. In the shadows, he could still see her on the beach and it was as if sharp talons had shredded what was left of his heart. 'Turn on the lamp,' he snapped out.

He felt the mattress dip and the room filled with a soft rosy light, chasing away the shadows and images. He blinked awake, desperate not to see her falling back into that hell hole.

And then the words, the pain, the memories were tumbling out. 'We were attacked by an unseen enemy on a beach. My youngest recruit was killed. I was in charge, I was the one responsible. It should've been me who died that day.'

'Oh, Blake.' She brushed her fingers over his brow. 'Why would you say that about yourself? It shouldn't have been anyone. Let me in...please.'

He turned and looked at her. 'You're a good listener, Lissa. The only one who ever listened.' The only woman who ever cared what was inside him.

She stared down at him, her eyes wide and full of compassion. 'Start at the beginning and don't stop till you're through.'

He put a hand behind his head and stared at the ceiling. Then he took a deep breath. 'We were on a routine training exercise...'

Lissa's heart wept for him as he told her, his gaze fixed on horrors she couldn't see.

'I woke up in a military hospital,' he said at last.

'Thank God,' she whispered.

'They called me a hero.' He drove a hand over his head. 'If I'd been doing my job right I'd've seen the signs earlier and Torque might still be alive today.'

'No. You did what you could. No one could have done more. You're a good, good man, Blake. The best. You couldn't save Torque, but you've done so much for others. You've spent years protecting our country. Protecting us. Think about Gilda. And me—think about all you've done for me. The boat. *Your* boat. You never told Jared the story behind that, did you? The business you've helped me build. Todd.

'Forgive yourself, Blake. Let me help you.' She closed his eyelids gently with her fingertips. 'Sleep now. I'll be here.'

[faint mirrored text from previous page bleeding through]

CHAPTER FOURTEEN

'I SHOULD'VE bought a new dress.' Lissa surveyed her reflection, less than satisfied. It was her big night and her little black dress was strapless and short and simple. Everyone else would be blinged to the eyeballs and the party princess was a plain Jane. But she hadn't had time to wander the boutiques.

'That is a new dress,' Blake said, behind her.

'And that is such a typical male response.' She glanced at Blake in the mirror to check he was okay after finally opening up to her last night.

He was buttoning his shirt. Covering all that gorgeous bronze skin. He looked amazing. Semi relaxed. She knew he wasn't looking forward to facing a crowd of people. She stared back at herself. 'It's not what I imagined myself wearing tonight. I look so…stark. And boring. Maybe a brighter lip-gl—'

'Perhaps these will help.' Blake's reflection appeared behind her. He lifted his hands above her head and she saw a single strand of cream pearls.

'Oh…' She met his eyes in the mirror—warm and incredibly blue, like a tropical day, and for a heart-stopping moment she forgot to breathe.

Then he broke eye contact, as if he'd seen something he wasn't comfortable with. 'Lift your hair.'

Unable to speak for the lump in her throat, she did as he

asked. He fastened it around her neck, then adjusted its princess length so that the diamond-crusted clasp sat below the line of her collarbones. It sparked like fire in the bedroom light.

'Oh, my…I don't know what to say.' She touched the smooth orbs, cool against her suddenly flushed skin. They must have cost a fortune. 'They're beautiful. And absolutely perfect.'

'They match your complexion.' His hands drifted over her bare shoulders as he turned her to face him, dropped a kiss on her brow. 'Good luck for tonight. You deserve it.'

'Thank you, Blake.' In turn, she leaned in to press her lips lightly against his neck just above his collar. 'For everything.'

But as she walked out into the night with him, something shivered down her spine. Hadn't she read somewhere that when a man gave a woman pearls, tears weren't far behind?

By eight-thirty the vaulted room where Lissa's Interior Design was to open for business on Monday morning was a sensory hive. Animated conversation. A fortune in fashion and fragrance and diamonds. Exotically perfumed pine-cone ginger stalks and Singapore orchids among tropical foliage. Colourful canapés, pink champagne. And over it all, the sounds of Vivaldi drifting from a quartet on the mezzanine floor.

Lissa mingled with the guests. Some she knew, others she met for the first time. Gilda, with her rapidly growing baby bump swathed in midnight blue, introduced her around. Blake was working the room from the opposite end.

Suddenly, she was enveloped in a tight warm hug and a familiar voice over her shoulder said, 'Hello, gorgeous.'

'Jared!' She turned in the circle of his arms and hugged him tight. 'I didn't know you were back.'

'We wanted to surprise you.'

'You did.' And for a moment she wanted to cling, to breathe

in his familiar aftershave and tell him she loved him, how much she appreciated him.

How much family meant to her even though she didn't always show it.

'Missed you,' she said, against his cheek.

'Same goes. Don't worry, sis,' he whispered for her ears only. 'I'm not going to rain on your parade.'

'I know. Thanks.'

He let her go and she stepped back, feeling unaccountably emotional. 'Sophie. You've cut your hair. It looks stunning.'

Sophie, gorgeous in a teal-coloured dress, flicked at her new bob with a smile. 'Easier to manage when travelling.'

'Crystal.' Lissa hugged them both. 'Thanks for coming. And Ian too. You all made it.' She soaked in the sight with all her senses. Her family loved her and they'd always be there for her, no matter what. They'd always be around to celebrate her successes.

She tried *not* to think about her business partner but her hand rose to the pearls at her neck. Blake would never be part of her inner circle. He wouldn't be here with champers when the business turned a profit for the first time. He wouldn't be here when it came time to decorate the office with Christmas cheer. He wouldn't be here to share their milestones *because he sailed alone.*

'Are you all right, Lissa?' Sophie asked, with a small frown.

'Are you kidding? With all this happening?' Waving an encompassing hand, she shook off the melancholy and smiled. 'Where are the kids?'

'Ian's parents are baby-sitting the lot,' Crystal said, then grinned. 'Overnight. So we're all staying at the Oceans Blue.' She glanced at Jared as she said, 'We're hoping you and Blake will join us for brunch tomorrow morning before we head back.'

'Love to. I'll ask Blake when I can catch him.' She glanced

about her. She'd hardly seen her partner in crime since they'd arrived. She saw him among the crowd, conversing with an elderly couple beneath the 'rings of fire', which they'd taken to calling the magnificent circles of light above them.

Her heart leapt against her breast at that first glimpse. It always did. It always would. The tanned skin and glossy dark hair, those brilliant blue eyes that she just wanted to drown in. His smile. He was smiling now as he talked, that delicious mouth kicked up at one corner, one hand holding a champagne flute, the other gesticulating as he made a point. Even though she knew he'd prefer to be alone or perhaps with her on some secluded moonlit beach.

But it wasn't only his physical beauty she saw. She saw the man behind the masculine perfection. A wounded man who'd only just begun to open up to her. His troubled family history.

She also knew him as a man of patience, understanding and integrity. He put up with the chaos she'd turned his house into with her work gear and her seeming inability to leave a room tidy.

He'd drawn out her deepest fears and soothed them with a gentleness she'd never have expected a man of his solitary background to be capable of.

But she kept the knowledge and her feelings deep. They'd agreed that if a more suitable partner came along, he'd be happy to bow out of the whole deal. More than happy, Lissa knew. He'd talked about sailing. He'd found a boat he was interested in. She knew he was leaving, it was only a matter of time.

Would he change his mind and stay if he knew she loved him?

Would it be fair to lay that on him?

No. Because with the emotional baggage he carried, to him they'd be empty words. And what would be the point? He didn't want to be tied to one place and she wanted this business so badly her eyeballs ached. They could never be together long term.

Jared's voice sounded over the microphone set up in the middle of the room, jerking her out of her thoughts. The guests quietened and gathered around.

'Ladies and gentlemen, welcome to Lissa's Interior Design.' Her brother smiled her way as the onlookers clapped. Emotion choked her. She lifted a hand in acknowledgement. She glanced at Blake but his attention was focused on Jared. She tried to interpret his expression without success.

When the applause settled down, Jared continued. 'Gilda's asked me to say a few words and I'm going to start by telling you about my kid sister...'

A few moments later, he finished by saying, 'And now with great pleasure and no small amount of pride, I want to introduce the talented woman who's going to transform your homes into magazine-worthy masterpieces. Lissa Sanderson, ladies and gentlemen.'

He handed her the mike, with a murmured 'Congratulations, sis,' and a brotherly pat on the back.

She clenched one hand around the microphone. 'Thank you, Jared.' Her voice resounded through the room. She blew him a kiss on a wide smile. 'That was quite a speech.' She glanced down at the scrap of paper in her hand.

'First off, I'd like to thank you all for coming and making the evening such a success...'

Crossing his arms, Blake stood well back from the crowd, out of the spotlight, and watched the exchange of fond smiles between the siblings. And an odd sensation tugged at him. He felt as if he were standing on a ship's splintering deck watching the rest of the crew cram into the only lifeboat and sail away. He tried to shake it away, but the feeling persisted.

She continued her speech but he wasn't listening to the words, he was listening to her voice—clear and crisp and calm, like the sound of a church bell over still water at sunset.

He couldn't take his eyes off her. The scrawny little red-head now the voluptuous Titian-haired beauty in a short black dress and taking on the world of interior decorating. If she'd left him at sea all those years ago, it was nothing to what she was doing to him now. He could imagine her in ten years. Twenty.

And she'd still be the only woman he wanted to look at.

'As most of you would already know, the evening's not just about Lissa's Interior Design. It's also about charity. Tonight I want to pay tribute to the men and women in the Armed Forces. Our own Aussie Diggers...'

Then those crystal clear eyes looked right at him. As if she'd known exactly where he was. In some still-functioning corner of his brain he registered her recognition to his line of work, even though he'd barely scratched the surface of that aspect of his life with her. With any woman.

'For those of you who haven't heard of it, the 'Support our Diggers' campaign provides health care, counselling and legal support for our troops overseas and for returned soldiers.

'Each and every one of them makes a huge personal sac-rifice to protect us here in Australia. They leave their fami-lies and loved ones and endure life-threatening situations on a daily basis. Some pay the ultimate price. Others return, changed for ever.'

Changed for ever. The words reverberated in his skull. Lissa had changed him. For the better. She'd shown him a different view of the world. One he liked. One he wanted. He rubbed a fist over his chest. Something was shifting inside him.

'So we want to champion the very worthy and valuable charity, 'Support our Diggers'. Make sure you see our char-ity diva, Gilda, and donate as much as you can before you leave.

'There's someone else, someone special, I want to ac-knowledge. Blake Everett. Most of you will remember Blake's mother, Rochelle, who worked tirelessly for charity from Surfers to the Sunshine Coast. Blake's the man responsible for making this dream of mine happen.'

Blake barely heard the resounding applause over the roaring in his ears.

I've been waiting my whole life for you.

He didn't know what to do with the feelings crashing around him. He'd heard her tell Jared what they had was a fling. *A wild, crazy no-strings affair with no unrealistic expectations.*

He needed to get outside, breathe some fresh air and think, because maybe this was the most important question he was ever going to ask himself, but before he could make his getaway a hand clapped his shoulder. 'Long time, no see, my friend.'

Blake turned at the voice and curbed his impatience. Jared's eyes pierced his as Blake extended a hand. 'Jared. It's good to see you.'

Jared nodded. 'Thanks for your phone call. It was reassuring to know Liss really wanted me here that badly.'

'You mean the world to her. Even if she doesn't always show it.'

'Same goes.' Jared cleared his throat. 'I want to thank you for helping her out with the boat.'

'Not a problem.'

'And with the business. I'd have helped but she's got that stubborn streak a mile wide.'

Blake felt a smile tug at his mouth. 'Believe me, I've seen it.'

She was also loyal and caring and all-the-way committed to making this venture a success, something he'd not been sure about at the start.

He looked about him, at the amazing job she'd done in transforming the building in such a short time. 'She's got talent and a good opportunity here. She'll do well.'

When he looked back, Big Brother was still watching him. 'So, what are your plans now?'

Blake heard the question behind the casual tone. And Lissa's words to Jared: *He'll be gone before you know it.* 'I've negotiated the price on a sailing yacht. Thought I'd sail north first and check out the Barrier Reef and the islands up there. Take in some diving. Recreational for a change.' He heard himself reciting the words as if from a dry school text. Why didn't he sound more enthusiastic? He'd been thinking about this for over a year, planning it for weeks.

'And the business?'

Lissa had always known how it would play. They'd both known. 'If she needs some advice and I'm out of contact—'

'She'll be just fine.' Jared watched him. 'She's got her family's support.'

Family. Yes, Lissa needed family. A house and a husband all the way committed. To settling down, raising her own kids.

'Blake...' A female of indeterminate age excused herself for interrupting but she'd known his mother...

Jared left them at some point and Blake was caught up with guests, then Gilda took the mike and proposed a toast. And everyone looked towards the spiral staircase where Lissa stood halfway up with a huge pair of gold scissors with purple foil streamers dangling from them. She cut a ribbon and a rainbow of balloons and foil confetti drifted down from the ceiling.

Cameras flashed, glasses clinked. Everyone cheered and clapped. Except Blake. Forget Helen of Troy, he thought as he watched her. Lissa's smile could launch a thousand ships ten times over.

As the metallic confetti swirled down around her, she locked eyes with him and it was like being sucked into a whirlpool of wants and needs and hopes, his or hers, he didn't know whose—just that they pulled him in a direction he'd never had any intention of going.

And all he knew was that he wanted to follow wherever it led. As she descended the steps he made his way towards her, his heart thumping like a piston in his chest. He didn't want to be a silent partner. He wanted a full partnership. So he didn't know much about interior decorating but he could learn, couldn't he? They could learn together. She could be the creative genius and he'd... They'd figure something out. But first he had to know how she felt. How she *really* felt about the two of them. Together.

She waved and headed straight for him, her smile glowing. 'I've got such exciting news.' She grabbed his arm. 'I'll tell you on the way...there's a party at Brandy's house and...' She trailed off, her brow creasing. 'You haven't got a headache, have you? You look pale...'

'I'm fine, in fact I—'

'So you'll come? Please, please, Blake, I want you there with me.'

'I need to talk to you first.'

'What about?'

'Not here.' He gestured with his chin. 'Outside.' Without waiting for a response, he took her elbow, and guided her past the crowd and out to the footpath. The sea air laden with the aromas of Asian stir fry and warm bitumen met them. He turned her towards him. 'Lissa, I—'

'Can it wait?' She all but jiggled on the spot, her beautiful face brimming with delight, clear eyes sparkling. 'The party's for—'

'This is important.' He grasped her upper arms, suddenly desperate.

'So is my career. Didn't you say to focus on my career first? Okay, I can't wait, I'll just have to spill it now...' She clasped her hands together beneath her chin, her eyes sparking with life and energy, bits of foil glinting in her hair. 'Maddie Jenkins wants in on the business as a full partner! You wouldn't be aware but she's got interior design shops all the way down the coast from Cairns to Brisbane and she wants Lissa's to be a part of it.'

Inside, Blake turned to stone. He loosened his hold. Who the hell was Maddie Jenkins? 'You haven't discussed it with me.' His lips felt numb; he felt as if someone else were pushing out the cool, clipped words. 'It's good manners to discuss any changes with your current partner first, don't you think?'

She stilled. 'Oh, Blake. I should have, I'm sorry. But it just happened moments ago.'

Her smile faded and the sparks in her eyes changed and he hated himself for being the cause but he couldn't find it in him to accept her apology.

When he didn't respond, she continued, 'You and I...we agreed it was a temporary arrangement until I found another interested party. Maddie's got years of experience and contacts all over the country. It'll still be Lissa's Interior Designs but this arrangement is just...so perfect. For me...*and* for you.'

Her eyes changed again, shadows stealing the light, but they remained level on his. 'You never really wanted to be involved in an interior design business. You only did it to help me out, we both know that. Because you knew I wouldn't accept charity. But you believed in me and I'll never forget it.'

He tightened his jaw. She was right, all the way right. 'You've got it all figured out.'

'It makes sense—for both of us. You're free now. Totally free. You can go off and do what you want, wherever you want. If that's what you want...'

'If I asked you to, would you come with me?' The words spilled out before he could stop them.

'What?' For a heartbeat he saw a flash of something like yearning in her eyes and his heart skipped a beat. 'Where? When?'

'Anywhere. Everywhere.' *For as long as for ever.*

'Why?' she asked quietly.

And he knew it wouldn't work, even if her eyes were telling him something else. Her new business was where she needed to be. She'd regret it for the rest of her life. Because he couldn't be the man she needed. He couldn't give her the kind of life she wanted.

So he shrugged as if his gut weren't tearing him up. *A moment of madness.* 'I just wanted to satisfy myself that you really are committed to this venture.'

She nodded, crossed her arms over her chest. 'And now you know. I can't believe you'd think I'd give up my career on a whim. You made this chance possible and I've worked towards it for so long. I'm going to take Maddie's offer while it's still on the table.' She searched his eyes for the longest time, as if committing them to memory.

He was vaguely aware that a group of younger party-goers stepped onto the footpath, that someone called her name. Still watching him, Lissa backed away towards them. Someone put a glass of champagne in her hand. She didn't seem to notice. 'You sure you won't come with us?'

He shook his head, barely managed a quick smile. 'Go do your thing, party girl. I've got some business of my own to take care of.'

'Someone'll drop me off, so I'll see you back at home, then.' She lifted her glass in a kind of salute.

Home? She'd never referred to his house as home before and warmth flickered deep inside only to cool instantly as he watched her walk away, his jaw so tight he wondered that he didn't crack a tooth.

Then she seemed to change her mind. She turned around and ran back, clutched at his shirt and blinked up at him. And for a pulse-pounding second a new dawn beckoned.

'Thank you, Blake, you're the best partner I ever had.' She reached up, pulled his head down and pressed her warm lips to his. The cold bubbly spilled out of her glass and down his shirt.

He pulled her closer, skimming the edge of something that felt eerily like panic. He'd faced enemy fire, unexploded mines and been life-threateningly close to running out of oxygen in the ocean's depths and always kept his cool. Used reasoning and logic to see him through.

There was nothing cool or reasonable or logical here.

When she broke the kiss and eased her heels back down to the footpath, the feeling didn't go away. It deepened.

She smiled and stepped back. 'The cleaning crew'll lock up when they're done.'

He jutted his chin towards the group up ahead. 'Your friends are waiting.'

She nodded. ''Night.' *Don't wait up*. He swore he heard those words on the balmy salt air.

CHAPTER FIFTEEN

HE SHOULD have enjoyed coming home alone. That was what he wanted, right? His temples throbbed with tension. Not wanting the light's harsh glare, Blake walked through the darkened house. The silence was shattering. He stopped outside Lissa's bedroom. The subtle fragrance she wore lingered on the air. He stepped through the doorway and looked about. It was the usual disaster area. A jumble of clothes, boxes, shopping bags.

Her presence extended to other rooms. Where she stored—and he used the word loosely—her tools of trade, where she sketched. Even his room didn't escape unscathed. Make-up and hair products. Her two pillows propped at a crazy angle against his headboard.

Damn. He'd become accustomed to it. It was…comfortable. Too comfortable.

His gaze moved to a photo he'd snapped of the two of them at the Loo with a View, a popular local spot overlooking the esplanade. She'd framed it for him to take with him when he left.

Their relationship had never been anything other than temporary. No misunderstanding on that score. It had been fun while it lasted.

Stretching out on the bed, he tucked her pillows behind his head. *Waiting for Lissa to come home.* What if…?

In his mind's eye he saw Lissa setting a birthday cake glowing with candles in front of him. Gifts on the sideboard. Smiling faces around the table. Jokes and laughter. Sharing his special day. Being part of a family. Shaking his head, he dismissed it before it could seize his heartstrings and never let go.

He'd made her, and himself, a commitment to stay, or at least remain in contact until Lissa was on her feet and able to manage without him. They'd come to that point. Closing his eyes, he made a mental list of all he needed to do.

Lissa quietly let herself in as the first line of scarlet smeared the sea's horizon. She grimaced as the door squeaked on its hinges. She hadn't meant to be out so late but she and Maddie had had a lot to discuss and the time had flown by. She'd texted Blake over two hours ago and left a message to tell him she was okay but she'd had no response.

Now the festivities and celebrations were over, everything else came flooding back. Fatigue hit her like a bomb. Not wanting to wake Blake, she slipped off her shoes, crept to the staircase and sat on the bottom step.

If I asked you to, would you come with me?

And for a moment there, at the party, looking into his eyes, she'd wavered. To sail with him off into the sunset. To live and love and grow old together. Her heart had yearned with the beauty of it, cried with the pain of it.

But he'd thrown it out there to test her *commitment*. Her sense of *responsibility*. To see if she was as good as her word.

So she'd given all the right reasons, all the logical reasons why she should say no. She'd struggled for independence most of her life and Lissa's Interior Designs was her passport.

But deep inside, where reason didn't exist, she'd wept.

Gathering up her shoes, she climbed the stairs. Blake's bedroom door was part-way open.

Suddenly unsure, she tapped before entering and was met by a brooding man with a surly tone. 'Morning, party girl.' He wore the same black jeans and ratty T-shirt he'd had on the night he'd landed on her deck. His hair had grown in the weeks since, and was furrowed now, as if he'd been running his hands through it. There were dark smudges beneath his eyes.

'I texted you,' she said.

One glance at the bed and she saw he was packing. Packing? Now? Swift and devastating pain stabbed at her. She'd known it was coming, but today?

'Yeah. Thanks for letting me know.' He folded T-shirts, laid them in his bag. 'So, you and Maddie got it all sorted?'

She barely heard him. 'You're leaving.'

'It's time. You've got what you wanted and my boat's been ready for a week. I'm picking it up tomorrow. I wanted to wait until the launch was over. Didn't want to spoil the fun.'

Her brain whirled with the shock and the details that needed sorting. 'Your loan. We have to arrange—'

'I don't need the money, Lissa. Keep it as a gift. I'll arrange for the paperwork.' He moved to the wardrobe and pulled shirts off hangers.

'I can't do that, it's not right. And it doesn't sit well with me. You know it doesn't.'

'Then donate it to the charity of your choice.'

'What about the house?' She'd need to find somewhere else to live.

He didn't look at her as he folded each shirt with the same precise care, laid it on the pile. 'There are no bookings for the next couple of months. I've just emailed the agent and informed him you're here for as long as you need to be. Till you find somewhere decent that you can afford.'

'I can't stay here.' *You're all around me.*

'Then do me a favour and house-sit for a while. It's always safer when someone's living in a place. And for God's sake stop telling me you can't. I know you can, and it's really not a word I want to hear right now.' Jaw tight, he slammed the bag's lid down, wrenched the zip closed.

He looked at her and his eyes did that magic thing she'd seen on rare occasions. They turned from hard flint to the softest tropical blue, just for an instant before reverting to hard once more. 'I need to leave. And it has to be now.' His voice was scratchy and raw, as if he'd swallowed sandpaper. 'Do you understand?'

No. 'No. I *don't* understand.' The full impact had taken a few moments to sink in and now shock turned to desperation. But she kept her voice steady. 'I do understand you need time to heal. But I can help you with that. Now you've talked about it, we can work on strategies together. If you want, we can see a counsellor…'

He shook his head. 'It was always temporary, Lissa. We knew that.'

'So that's it, then.' No tears. Her eyes were as dry as dust and she was grateful for it. A swift clean break now would allow her to focus on her new career. She'd be so busy she wouldn't have time to miss him.

'Why don't you go make us some breakfast?'

She couldn't seem to drag her eyes away from his face. This was what he wanted and she so wanted him to be happy. He deserved to be happy, to live his life in peace and solitude if that was what he wanted. But why did it have to hurt so much? Why did it feel as if her very soul were being torn apart?

'So you're walking away.' She'd sworn she'd not say it but it was as if someone else were speaking through her. 'After everything I've just said. After all we've been through. What we've come to mean to each other. You can pack up and move on *just like that*?' She clicked her fingers in front of her face.

And for one thudding heartbeat she thought she saw the same emotions rip through his gaze, but maybe she was hallucinating because when she blinked her vision clear there was nothing but that flinty-eyed, self-contained remoteness.

'On second thought, forget breakfast, it's best if I just go,' he said, with that same wretched aloofness. 'You're dead on your feet and you always did have that flair for the overly dramatic.'

He crossed to her, took her hands in his and she wanted to pull away from his touch, to prove she could, but her hands were numb. 'It's not the end of the world, Lissa, it's just the beginning. You'll thank me later. A good eight hours' sleep and everything will fall into perspective. You'll wake rejuvenated and ready to take on the next challenge in your life.

'We want different things. You need stability. A home, family. I want to feel the salt air on my face and drop anchor wherever I please. And that's not the kind of man you need. We had some good times but we always knew it was just a fling.'

She flinched at his tone and the word. *Fling*. It sounded almost sordid, an abomination for what she thought they'd had. Had she been the only one to feel that intensity? Or the only one dumb enough, naïve enough to let it matter?

'You know something? I don't *need a man* in my life. Why do you men always think you're so indispensable?'

'I guess we've said it all, then.' He picked up one of his bags, slung it over his shoulder.

'I guess we have.' Damn him, she wasn't going to watch him walk away. Their talk had drained every last drop of energy from her and she didn't know how much longer she could remain standing. 'I hope you enjoy your freedom. And I'll always be grateful for your helping hand when I was down, so thank you for that.' She stepped away. 'I think I'll go take that nap. You'll probably be gone when I wake up, so...I'll say goodbye now.'

He nodded once, then tore what was left of her heart out when he kissed her cheek lightly and said, 'I'll see you around some time.'

Not in this lifetime, she vowed later sitting on the couch with her arms around his pillow watching the afternoon shadows creep over the pool.

And she'd been left to explain why *he* wasn't going to be coming to brunch with her family. She'd opted out too, pleading fatigue. She squeezed her eyes shut to stop the tears.

In one evening she'd been handed her dream career, her independence, her new life. And lost the man she loved.

The shop opened on Monday. Jill, one of Maddie's staff from the Noosa branch, had come down to help for a couple of weeks with a view to looking at relocating there to be closer to her family. Older than Lissa and with a few years' experience under her belt, Jill was bright and enthusiastic and Lissa hoped she'd stay on.

People dropped in to wish Lissa well and share the bubbly Maddie had sent. She didn't think about Blake *at all*. No way. Not for a minute.

She did *not* imagine him sharing the excitement of her first day or seeing him walk in at closing, eyes hot for her, hair glinting under the rings of fire when he came to whisk her away for a celebration dinner.

Then mid-morning a massive floral arrangement arrived. Three dozen fragrant yellow roses spilling from a ginormous glass bowl. 'Someone loves you.' Jill grinned as the black-capped delivery guy in his crisp black shirt with its gold logo set it on the coffee table in the display area.

A little tag gave instructions for care of cut flowers and a hand-written explanation that yellow roses celebrated success and new beginnings.

'My brother.' Lissa smiled back, tugging at the attached

envelope. 'He's always...' Her voice trailed off, her smile dropping away as she read the card inside.

Congratulations! Thinking of you today. Blake.

The surprise caught her off-guard. Her nose stung, her eyes brimmed and something huge and heavy lodged in her throat. He'd thought enough to choose the exact right flowers and, what was more, he'd wanted her to know. 'They're from my... They're from Blake.'

'You mean that dishy navy guy from Saturday night?'

Lissa heard Jill's appreciative murmur and shuffled the card quickly back in its envelope. 'He's left the navy. Bought himself a yacht. He won't be coming back any time soon.' She turned her back on the flowers and headed for her desk, aware of Jill's gaze boring into her neck.

But she slept in his bed that night. The following night she moved her stuff there. Just for the short time until she found her own place. She told herself she liked the view of the river from there.

In the evenings after putting in hours of overtime at Lissa's, she sketched. She finished the piece she'd been working on. After all, she knew every plane and angle of his face. A portrait of Blake. She'd give it to him some time when he was passing through.

She put on some music and danced in the living room until she was physically exhausted, then tossed for hours, unable to sleep. Citing work as the reason, she put off visiting her family.

Work, work, work. It gave her a reason to get up in the morning. She enjoyed the long hours. She loved seeing the process move from plan to finished perfection. The income allowed her to start repaying the debt into the bank account Blake had set up.

To her surprise, over the next few weeks she discovered she could live without Blake and not fall to pieces every time she thought of him. She knew she could lead the fulfilling, independent life she'd wanted.

But now she knew Blake as well as anyone could, she'd always feel as if a part of her were missing. One day she might even be able to think about dating again. It was ironic that it had been Blake who'd given her back that confidence.

She'd not heard a single solitary word from him, nor had she contacted him. She told herself it was better that way. One email or text, one phone call and she'd want more.

Blake didn't.

Blake cradled his mug of tea while he watched the sun lift out of the water. It swam on the horizon, a ball of fire shimmering in the early morning haze. Fingers of crimson spread along the yacht's decking and stroked his skin with sultry warmth. The air was thick with humidity and the smell of the ocean, the way he liked it.

To his right, tropical rainforest capped a steep peak, then dipped all the way down to a golden ribbon of sand. If he looked to his left he could see the conical shape of one of the Barrier Reef's unspoiled islands rising out of an indigo and turquoise sea.

This was paradise.

Who wouldn't give their all to be in his place right now? He breathed deep as he watched a flock of seabirds dip and dive, and took a bite out of his toasted bacon sandwich. The water lapped at the hull, the sails flapped lazily.

This was freedom.

He could take the time to enjoy the wind in his hair and the sun on his back. No one to tell him what to do and how to do it. No one to tell him when to get up, where to go.

No one.

He shook off the edgy feeling. He wasn't lonely. He could drop anchor at the nearest marina any time and chat with the locals at the yacht club. He didn't need company.

Why waste time building relationships that always ended? Why build a home, settle in one place when he could take his seafaring home anywhere he wanted?

This was living the dream.

All he needed was a seaworthy boat, food on his plate and a comfortable bed. He curled both palms around the railing. All he wanted was peace and solitude and a blue horizon.

The hell it was.

One night after she'd closed up, Lissa looked at a tiny apartment that was becoming available at the end of the following month. No sea views but she couldn't afford to be choosy. She drove home feeling happier than she had in a while.

As she pulled into the driveway she saw a stretched limo out the front of Gilda's house. Off to one of her charity events, no doubt.

It wasn't until she was walking along the path to the front door that she heard the footsteps behind her.

'Ms Sanderson?'

'Yes?' She turned as the uniformed driver approached and it occurred to her that she'd felt none of that tingling alarm that had dogged her for so long.

'Good evening.' He took off his chauffeur's cap. He was medium height with an easy smile and greying hair and he handed her his ID. 'My name's Max Fitzgerald and I've been asked to give you this package then wait until you're ready. I'm to transport you to your dinner meeting.' He handed her a large flat box.

She frowned at the ID. He appeared to be who it said he was. Should she be suspicious? 'I don't have a dinner appointment,' she said. 'I bought a frozen meal on the way home.'

'You didn't receive a text message explaining?'

Oh? 'I haven't checked, I've been…busy…' She fished in her handbag for her phone. The screen lit up at her touch and she opened the text.

Lissa, you can trust Max. It's time we discussed moving on with the rest of our lives.

She recognised Blake's number.

For a few stunned seconds she couldn't move. Then her heart flipped over and dropped like a stone. *Now* he wanted to talk? Just when she was getting used to not having him around?

He probably had tenants waiting to lease the house and wanted her to vacate. *He wanted to get on with the rest of his life.*

Or did he think that he could just turn up out of the blue and whistle—or text—and she'd come running? Other women might but not Lissa Sanderson. He couldn't even be bothered inviting her personally to have this discussion or collecting her himself?

'I'm not free tonight,' she told Max, slipping her phone back into her bag. 'I'll text him. Thanks, you can leave.'

'He told me you might say that. He asked me to beg you to reconsider.'

'I don't—'

'Please, Ms Sanderson.' Max ran his fingers over the cap in his hand. 'He asked me to get down on one knee if I had to and I'm getting too old for all that.' His eyes lit with humour. 'My joints aren't what they used to be.'

Lissa stared at him. Blake had begged? Pleaded? He wanted to see her that badly? A glimmer of something like hope flickered inside her but she pushed it down. 'There's no need for that.' She looked at the smooth, white, expensive-looking box in her hands. 'Why don't you come inside and I'll just see what's in this package…?'

'I'll wait in the vehicle, if that's all right with you, ma'am. Take your time, I'll be here till dawn.'

'Dawn?' Was he serious?

'Mr Everett explained you like to party on occasion.'

'Did he?' she murmured. Obviously he thought she'd got on with her life. She didn't know whether to be amused or offended. 'Okay, Max. I'll be sure to let you know my decision soon.'

The moment she was inside, Lissa pulled the string off the box. Her heart raced as her fingers scrabbled through the mountain of tissue paper.

A slimline gown of the palest aquamarine. It shimmered in the light as she drew it out. Or maybe it was the tears that sprang to her eyes making it seem so.

'Oh, my...goodness.' She'd never seen anything more exquisite.

Her arms shook as she held it against her. It flowed to the floor like a slender stream of clear spring water. Shoestring straps and a low back that dipped to her waist.

As she raced upstairs to try it on she didn't let herself think, dared not allow herself to hope.

CHAPTER SIXTEEN

MAX was out of the limo the moment she stepped through the front door twenty tension-fraught minutes later. 'Very becoming,' he said, nodding as she approached. 'You look lovely.'

'Thank you.' She smoothed a hand down the slippery fabric. It fitted like a dream. She wondered if that was what this was. Just a dream. Like the ones she'd had so many years ago.

He reached into the vehicle and withdrew a small bouquet of creamy gardenias and presented them to her as he opened her door.

'Oh...' She inhaled their delicate green fragrance. 'Thank you, again.'

She slid inside and set the flowers beside her on the soft leather seat. Through the speakers, Robbie was singing about angels. A bottle of champagne chilled in an ice-bucket beside a crystal flute.

'Can I pour you a glass of champagne before we leave?' Max asked.

'Oh, no.' She pressed a hand to her jittering stomach. 'I really couldn't.'

As they drew smoothly away from the kerb she tried to remember the last time she'd refused champagne. But right now her insides simply wouldn't tolerate it. And she needed a clear head to face Blake.

This might seem like a dream but she couldn't be sure it was the dream she wanted. Wouldn't allow herself to think beyond the next step. According to his text, he was expecting them to have a discussion. Over dinner. Maybe he liked women to look sophisticated when he dined. Or maybe... She shook her head and looked out at the darkening tropical sky with its anvil thunderheads building over the hinterland. She refused to contemplate any more maybes.

The journey took only a few minutes. At the Mooloolaba Marina she stepped into the deepening twilight, clutching her flowers and her bag.

Then Max was accompanying her through the security gate and towards a luxury yacht that dwarfed every other watercraft in the vicinity. Light spilled from the main deck and shimmered on the inky water. This wasn't the simple sailing boat she'd seen in Blake's brochure, even though that, too, had been a luxury in her eyes.

This was a floating palace. With its sleek white lines, it reminded her of a powerful beast waiting to be unleashed. She could visualise it slicing through the water with Blake at the helm. And that was probably where he'd be tomorrow, or the next day when his business with her was concluded.

And then she saw him. On the deck. In slim-fitting dark trousers and a white shirt open at the neck with the cuffs rolled back. Her heart stopped, then beat at double time. Their gazes met. Held for what seemed like eternity while the water lapped and the foody aroma from the nearby waterside restaurants wafted on the air. She could do this. She could.

Still watching her, he walked down the gangplank towards her. She could have a civilised meal then walk away...

'Good evening, Lissa.'

His tone was welcoming, if a little formal and, oh, how she'd missed that deep rich voice. But she could live without it. 'Hello.'

He barely glanced at the chauffeur. 'Thank you, Max. That'll be all for now.'

He reached out and sifted his fingers through the hair curling over her shoulders. She had time to breathe in his musky scent before he stepped back.

'Thank you for the dress. It's beautiful.'

'You make it so. And you're welcome.'

He leaned forward, touched cool dry lips to her cheek. Smooth skin. He'd shaved recently and smelled sinfully good for such a chaste kiss. She could feel the last of her strength draining out of her.

'I hope you haven't eaten already,' he said, placing a warm palm at the small of her bare back to guide her onto the boat.

She almost sighed at the contact before arching away and quickening her steps. She looked at the luxury surrounding her. 'This is a magnificent yacht.'

'I sold off most of my investments to buy it.'

She stared up at the stern's fibreglass U-shaped structure, which arched over a comfortable table setting with satin wicker chairs. Down-lights reflected on the table set for two with silver cutlery and white china. A candle glowed inside a tall glass.

Through a wide open doorway she could see a spacious living room. Thick blue carpet, polished wood and brass fittings, over-stuffed leather chairs and a bar with hidden lighting that sparkled with rows of bottles. 'This is all too overwhelming. You've been gone a month and now…'

'Twenty-six days, actually.'

She knew. Twenty-six days and thirteen hours.

A uniformed waiter appeared with a silver tray. Lissa recognised him from the catering company they'd used for the launch party.

'Would you care for a prawn tail with wasabi and lemon sauce?' Blake asked.

Her stomach writhed with nerves and nausea. She set her flowers on the table. 'I won't be dining with you. I came tonight because you went to such a lot of trouble to get me here, and I felt a little sorry for Max, but I need to know what you want. And I need to know now. Then I'll be leaving. We won't see each other again.'

Blake's demeanour changed. His jaw tightened and she saw his fingers flex at his sides. So his night wasn't going according to plan? Neither was hers.

He glanced at the waiter, waved him off. 'Take a break, Nathan.'

Lissa took the opportunity to move to the railing and looked out over the myriad boats bobbing on the water. From that distance she made herself turn to face him. And, oh, she wished she didn't have to because looking at him made her want to tell him things she knew he wouldn't want to hear.

'In your text you suggested moving on with our lives. I thought that's what we were doing.'

'I thought so too. Until a week ago.'

He took a step towards her but she held up a hand. 'Don't come any closer. Please, Blake.' She latched onto the only reason she could think of. 'You found someone to lease the house and you want me to vacate, right?'

He seemed to consider a moment. 'It's true, I want you to vacate the house.' His eyes were dark and steady on hers. 'Because I want you to live here on this boat. With me.'

The simplicity of his words—and the shock—pinned her feet to the deck. She gripped the railing for support. He wanted her to live with him. But he wanted it all his way. He was suggesting what was essentially a convenient live-in arrangement. She'd been there, done that, had the restraining order to prove it. No one was going to use her as a convenience again.

'We've played this scene before. I thought I already made it clear to you that I'm committed to my career—'

'I love you, Lissa.'

'That I—'

'I don't want to spend another day or another night without you.'

He took another step closer and this time she didn't try to stop him. Because she was too busy trying to breathe. To stay upright. To process the implications of what he was saying.

'And you think because you tell me you love me...' she hitched in a breath as she said the words and tightened her grip on the railing '...I'll give up all I've worked towards for you?'

'No.' His gaze reached out to her, holding her captive as he walked towards her. 'I'm going to stay here, in Mooloolaba, because here is where you are.'

What little breath she had left rushed out. She sucked in more salt-laden air. 'What happened to feeling the sea breeze in your face and dropping anchor wherever you please?'

'I thought that's what I wanted. But now I know I want you more.' He pushed a hand through his hair. 'For God's sake, Lissa, put me out of this hell I'm in and say yes. Tell me you love me back. Tell me what we had wasn't just a fling.'

She looked up at him, his face taut in the spill of light. She'd never seen such raw vulnerability in his face before. She'd never seen his expression so...open. 'I do love you,' she said softly. 'I always have and I always will. You were the one who always talked about leaving. And you were the one who called it a fling.'

'I heard you talking to Jared.'

Oh... And she felt a small smile touch her lips momentarily. 'Don't you know not to eavesdrop on private conversations?'

'Lissa...'

'It was never a fling, not to me. No, don't touch me.' She stepped away from his outstretched hand. 'Not yet. I want to know what made you come back.'

The haunted look she'd seen so often flickered behind his eyes. 'I realised I wanted to live before they bury me.'

'Torque…'

He nodded.

Then he didn't give her time to move. He gathered her up into his arms and held her close so she could hear his heart beating solidly beneath her ear. And she wanted to stay there in his safe and solid embrace for ever. He tucked her head beneath his chin and she knew he was looking out over the horizon.

'I felt his soul leave his body, Lissa, as I dragged him across the sand. I still hear the gunfire sometimes.'

'The nightmares…' Lissa whispered. 'You still have them.'

'Not as often.' He took a deep breath, stroked her hair. 'He was only eighteen. Thousands of miles from home. He'd barely begun to live and he was dead already.'

'I know.' She curled her hand against his heart. 'You need to learn to forgive yourself.'

'I'm working on it. I went to visit Torque's parents. They were so grateful there was someone with him when he passed. That he didn't suffer. It's helped. Both them and me.'

She nodded. 'I'm glad.'

He was silent a moment while the breeze blew over the deck. 'I came home to recuperate because I was looking for that familiarity I hadn't experienced in so long.

'I never expected to find you. A woman I could love. A love I can trust, a love I can give myself wholly to.'

Tears welled in her eyes and spilled over onto his shirt. He shifted so that he could cup her head in his hands, tilt it up and look into her eyes. 'A love that will last a lifetime.'

Her heart swelled to bursting. 'Blake…'

'I know you have your business and that I'm no longer a part of it, but that doesn't mean I can't be involved in some small way, does it?'

'Of course you c—'

'The marina's a few minutes' drive away from the shop. This yacht has more comfort and luxury than you've ever seen. You have Maddie and her team to help out now and then so when we want a weekend away we can just take off, up the coast, or down to Surfers to visit your family. The best of both worlds. The sea and, most importantly, you.'

Her thoughts were jumbled, spinning with the images he was conjuring with his words.

But he wasn't finished. He stepped back and drew something out of his pocket. He flipped the little velvet box open. 'Are you prepared to take on this scarred sailor who'll probably wake you up with bad dreams some nights?'

'Oh…I—'

'Marry me, Lissa. Live with me for the rest of our lives. Be my life's comfort and I'll be yours.'

Through her tears she saw a ring with a solitary aquamarine flanked by a diamond on either side. 'Oh…do you know how long I've waited to hear you ask that question?' she whispered. 'Fantasised where we'd be, how you'd ask? And it was never as perfect as this. And the answer is yes. A thousand times yes.'

'You're the only girl for me, Lissa. And I'll spend my life showing you.' He slid it onto the third finger of her left hand. 'A stone that captures the sea and the colour of your eyes. There's something of both of us in it.'

'It's beautiful,' she said softly. 'I couldn't have chosen anything better.' She watched it glitter in the light, then turned to him with a smile that came from the deepest corner of her heart. 'And now…are you going to seal this deal with a kiss?'

He smiled back and this time his amazing blue eyes were filled with sunshine and light. 'Try stopping me.'

And, oh, she'd missed his luscious mouth on hers. The taste of him, the scent of him as he drew her closer. Finally, he drew back and she knew it was only because they'd both run out of air.

'Now I want to show you your new home.'

He pulled his phone from his pocket. 'Max? We won't need your services for the rest of the night, thank you. Go home to bed.' He disconnected with a serious gleam in his eye. 'I intend to.'

Then he swept her up in his arms and carried her through the living room at a rate of knots. 'We'll do the more detailed tour later,' he told her, barely raising a puff. He paused at the galley's entrance to tell Nathan he could leave, that they'd help themselves to the meal later.

Then on through another entertainment area with wide-screen TV and concealed lighting that gave the room a pink-purple glow. Up the low polished wooden spiral staircase in the centre. Past a bathroom and its moulded spa bath with clear Perspex sides and marble vanity.

Blake set her on her feet in front of a massive double bed with a deep indigo quilt. Finally. He had her right where he wanted her. She glanced about her. 'I've got a really nice sketch that would suit this room...'

He could see her studying the décor with a trained eye. 'I think it's really you...'

'Not now, sweet cheeks.' He touched her chin and turned it so that she was looking at him. Only him. 'Take the night off.' His lips roamed her face while his hands moved over the delicate silk, reacquainting himself with her shape. Her fragrance. Her heat. 'I've missed you,' he murmured. It was a first for him. Hell, the whole evening had been about firsts.

He felt her smile against his mouth. 'So what have you missed about me?'

He kissed her again, then cupped her cheeks and looked into those clear sea-green eyes. 'I've missed your colour, your resilience. Your independence.' He punctuated each with a kiss. 'The way you listen when I talk, as if I matter. The way you push me to open up because you give a damn.'

He saw her eyes spring with moisture and smoothed the dampness away with his thumbs. 'I've even missed your chaos, believe it or not.'

'I've been trying to do something about that,' she whispered.

'Don't ever change. I love you just the way you are, feminine hygiene products on my bathroom shelf and all.'

He smoothed a hand over her breast so that he could feel her heart beating beneath his palm. 'You made me realise I've been existing but I've not been living. I've been hiding behind my navy career, too afraid to take another chance on love.'

'I was afraid too.' She closed her hand over his. Over her heart. 'You taught me to trust again.'

'I reckon we're pretty darn good for each other.'

'I reckon so. Except you forgot one thing.'

'Yeah?'

'You forgot how much you missed making love with me.'

'I didn't forget.' And he tumbled with her back onto the bed.

He was home.

* * * * *

CLASSIC

Quintessential, modern love stories
that are romance at its finest.

EXTRA

COMING NEXT MONTH from Harlequin Presents®
AVAILABLE JANUARY 31, 2012

**#3041 MONARCH OF
THE SANDS**
Sharon Kendrick

#3042 THE LONE WOLF
The Notorious Wolfes
Kate Hewitt

**#3043 ONCE A FERRARA
WIFE...**
Sarah Morgan

**#3044 PRINCESS FROM THE
PAST**
Caitlin Crews

**#3045 FIANCÉE FOR
ONE NIGHT**
21st Century Bosses
Trish Morey

**#3046 THE PETROV
PROPOSAL**
Maisey Yates

COMING NEXT MONTH from Harlequin Presents® EXTRA
AVAILABLE FEBRUARY 14, 2012

#185 ONE DESERT NIGHT
One Night In...
Maggie Cox

**#186 ONE NIGHT IN THE
ORIENT**
One Night In...
Robyn Donald

**#187 INTERVIEW WITH
THE DAREDEVIL**
Unbuttoned by a Rebel
Nicola Marsh

**#188 SECRET HISTORY OF
A GOOD GIRL**
Unbuttoned by a Rebel
Aimee Carson

You can find more information on upcoming Harlequin® titles,
free excerpts and more at www.HarlequinInsideRomance.com.

HPECNM0112

REQUEST YOUR FREE BOOKS!

◆Harlequin *Presents*~

PASSION GUARANTEED SEDUCTION

2 FREE NOVELS PLUS
2 FREE GIFTS!

YES! Please send me 2 FREE Harlequin Presents® novels and my 2 FREE gifts (gifts are worth about $10). After receiving them, if I don't wish to receive any more books, I can return the shipping statement marked "cancel." If I don't cancel, I will receive 6 brand-new novels every month and be billed just $4.30 per book in the U.S. or $4.99 per book in Canada. That's a saving of at least 14% off the cover price! It's quite a bargain! Shipping and handling is just 50¢ per book in the U.S. and 75¢ per book in Canada.* I understand that accepting the 2 free books and gifts places me under no obligation to buy anything. I can always return a shipment and cancel at any time. Even if I never buy another book, the two free books and gifts are mine to keep forever.   106/306 HDN FERQ

Name	(PLEASE PRINT)	

Address		Apt. #

City	State/Prov.	Zip/Postal Code

Signature (if under 18, a parent or guardian must sign)

Mail to the **Reader Service:**
IN U.S.A.: P.O. Box 1867, Buffalo, NY 14240-1867
IN CANADA: P.O. Box 609, Fort Erie, Ontario L2A 5X3

Not valid for current subscribers to Harlequin Presents books.

**Are you a current subscriber to Harlequin Presents books
and want to receive the larger-print edition?
Call 1-800-873-8635 or visit www.ReaderService.com.**

* Terms and prices subject to change without notice. Prices do not include applicable taxes. Sales tax applicable in N.Y. Canadian residents will be charged applicable taxes. Offer not valid in Quebec. This offer is limited to one order per household. All orders subject to credit approval. Credit or debit balances in a customer's account(s) may be offset by any other outstanding balance owed by or to the customer. Please allow 4 to 6 weeks for delivery. Offer available while quantities last.

Your Privacy—The Reader Service is committed to protecting your privacy. Our Privacy Policy is available online at www.ReaderService.com or upon request from the Reader Service.

We make a portion of our mailing list available to reputable third parties that offer products we believe may interest you. If you prefer that we not exchange your name with third parties, or if you wish to clarify or modify your communication preferences, please visit us at www.ReaderService.com/consumerschoice or write to us at Reader Service Preference Service, P.O. Box 9062, Buffalo, NY 14269. Include your complete name and address.

HPI1B

Louisa Morgan loves being around children.
So when she has the opportunity to tutor bedridden Ellie,
she's determined to bring joy back into the motherless
girl's world. Can she also help Ellie's father open his
heart again? Read on for a sneak peek of

THE COWBOY FATHER

by Linda Ford,
available February 2012 from Love Inspired Historical.

Why had Louisa thought she could do this job? A bubble of self-pity whispered she was totally useless, but Louisa ignored it. She wasn't useless. She could help Ellie if the child allowed it.

Emmet walked her out, waiting until they were out of earshot to speak. "I sense you and Ellie are not getting along."

"Ellie has lost her freedom. On top of that, everything is new. Familiar things are gone. Her only defense is to exert what little independence she has left. I believe she will soon tire of it and find there are more enjoyable ways to pass the time."

He looked doubtful. Louisa feared he would tell her not to return. But after several seconds' consideration, he sighed heavily. "You're right about one thing. She's lost everything. She can hardly be blamed for feeling out of sorts."

"She hasn't lost everything, though." Her words were quiet, coming from a place full of certainty that Emmet was more than enough for this child. "She has you."

"She'll always have me. As long as I live." He clenched his fists. "And I fully intend to raise her in such a way that even if something happened to me, she would never feel like I was gone. I'd be in her thoughts and in her actions every day."

Peace filled Louisa. "Exactly what my father did."

Their gazes connected, forged a single thought about fathers and daughters...how each needed the other. How sweet the relationship was.

Louisa tipped her head away first. "I'll see you tomorrow."

Emmet nodded. "Until tomorrow then."

She climbed behind the wheel of their automobile and turned toward home. She admired Emmet's devotion to his child. It reminded her of the love her own father had lavished on Louisa and her sisters. Louisa smiled as fond memories of her father filled her thoughts. Ellie was a fortunate child to know such love.

Louisa understands what both father and daughter are going through. Will her compassion help them heal—and form a new family? Find out in
THE COWBOY FATHER
by Linda Ford, available February 14, 2012.

Love Inspired Books celebrates 15 years of inspirational romance in 2012! February puts the spotlight on Love Inspired Historical, with each book celebrating family and the special place it has in our hearts. Be sure to pick up all four Love Inspired Historical stories, available February 14, wherever books are sold.

Harlequin®

n o c t u r n e™

NEW YORK TIMES AND *USA TODAY*
BESTSELLING AUTHOR

RACHEL LEE

captivates with another installment of

The Claiming

When Yvonne Dupuis gets a creepy sensation that
someone is watching her, waiting in the shadows,
she turns to Messenger Investigations and finds herself
under the protection of vampire Creed Preston.
His hunger for her is extreme, but with evil lurking
at every turn Creed must protect Yvonne from the
demonic forces that are trying to capture her
and claim her for his own.

CLAIMED BY A VAMPIRE

Available in February wherever books are sold.

HN61876